D1104908

ROSA AND MEE
Written by Ben Goldstein

TABLE OF CONTENTS

TABLE OF CONTENTS

To all my students and teachers

CHAPTER 1 – FIRE!

"Mami, Mami!"

Ten-year-old Rosa woke with a scream as a hot spark touched her cheek. Smoke filled the room from the cracks in the ceiling above her bed. She quickly jumped from her mattress to the floor as her quilt burst into flames and part of the ceiling came crashing down.

"Mami, Mami!"

Scared for her life, Rosa ran down the long, dark apartment hallway and burst through the doorway to her mother's room.

"Fire! Mami, FIRE!"

Rosa shook her mother, Luishana, awake, and pointed to the smoke now billowing through the hallway. Luishana jumped from her bed and pulled open the window to the fire escape. She turned and grabbed Jorge, her three-year-old son from his crib.

"Out! Out! Go! Go!"

Luishana pushed Rosa through the open window and onto the landing.

"Quickly, quickly. Andale! Hurry!"

As they descended the fire escape stairs, Luishana banged loudly on the windows of the other apartments. "Get up! Get up! Fire! Fire!"

The wail of fire engines echoed through the darkness.

Rosa was afraid but she imitated her mother and shouted as she passed each window.

"Get up! Get up! Fire! Fire!"

An elderly lady, Mrs. Hernandez, poked her head out of a third-floor window and pointing her cane at Rosa asked, "What's all the noise?"

Rosa pointed to the flames above. "The building is on fire. Come quickly."

Mrs. Hernandez disappeared inside her apartment and returned a moment later with a cat in her arms. "Take Sophie," she said and handed the cat to Rosa.

Rosa took hold of the cat with one hand and helped Mrs. Hernandez through the window with the other. She looked up. The top of the building was ablaze.

The rusty fire escape ladder made a gut-wrenching sound and jammed about eight feet off the ground. Luishana tried to lower it to street level. People streamed out of the nearby buildings, gathered in the street below, and watched as the first police cars arrived.

Luishana hung on to the fire escape ladder with one arm, held Jorge with the other, and lowered him into the outstretched arms of an old man in the crowd below. She next lowered Rosa and Sophie the cat to safety. Mrs. Hernandez stood on the flight above, frozen in fear. Luishana bounded up the steps to the old woman, who protested going any further.

"I can't! I can't!"

"Dios! Come! Come!" cried Luishana.

Smoke and flames filled the sky from the windows above them as Luishana shepherded the old lady down the last few steps of the fire escape. A muscular young man from the street grabbed the rungs of the fire escape ladder and swung up to assist Luishana. Together they lowered the old woman into the street. Finally, Luishana hung from the ladder and jumped to safety, scraping her knees on the ground.

The firefighters unwrapped their hoses and began to battle the flames. Ladders were raised. An ambulance arrived. Rosa, Luishana, Jorge, Mrs. Hernandez, and Sophie, her cat, sat huddled together in the chill of the night, as the blaze was subdued. An emergency medical worker came over and offered them warm blankets. Still in their pajamas and nightgowns, they wrapped the blankets around themselves to protect themselves from the cold.

CHAPTER 2 - SCHOOL

The school term had started. The already overworked secretarial staff at P.S. 101 was trying to deal with the chaos of the first days of school. Rosa, her mother, and her baby brother waited patiently and finally caught the attention of Mrs. Gomez, the school secretary.

"Can, I help you?"

Luishana produced a note that she handed to Mrs. Gomez.

"Yes, they said we should come here. This is my daughter, Rosa."

Mrs. Gomez looked at the note and then at Rosa. "I know Rosa," said Ms. Gomez. "She was here last year."

Luishana smiled, "Yes."

"You'll need to fill out this change of address form," said Mrs. Gomez. She pointed to the lines on the form and translated the terms into Spanish.

"Your name here. Address. Telephone Number."

"I don't have a telephone. I lost it in the fire. We're staying in a shelter. The guard has a number,"said Luishana.

"Just write that number," said the school secretary.

"It's a shelter on 101st Street. Our apartment burned down. Will Rosa still be able to go to school here?"

"Yes, I think so."

Mrs. Gomez looked at the schedule of kids and classes on the countertop.

"She was assigned to Mr. Villa's class. Room 219. You know where that is, Rosa?"

Rosa nodded yes.

"I'll give you a note and you can go right up."

Luishana smiled and hugged Rosa.

Note in hand, Rosa walked down the long empty hallway and opened the door to Mr. Villa's classroom. She stood silently in the doorway. Mr. Villa was a young, macho ex-Marine who had decided to make teaching his career. This was his first year at P.S. 101, and it was a challenge. Turning from the class, he noticed Rosa shyly waiting to be acknowledged.

"Come in. Is that note for me?" said Mr. Villa.

Rosa nodded and handed him the note.

"What's your name?"

"Rosa."

"Okay, Rosa, take a seat over there, next to Luis."

Rosa walked over to the empty desk, which Mr. Villa indicated, and sat down. She looked at Luis and tried to smile and say hi, but the boy seemed extremely bashful. Luis took a quick peek at Rosa and then quickly looked away.

CHAPTER 3 - THE PLAYGROUND

Recess at P.S.101 was often disorderly and raucous. Kids chased each other running wildly around the playground till a teacher interceded or a whistle was blown. Boys played tag, wrestled, played basketball, and threw balls around the yard. Some of the girls jumped rope, Double Dutch style. Rosa tagged along with Latoya and Serena, two girls from her fourth-grade class. Luis, who usually stayed by himself, decided to follow, sat down by the fence, and watched the girls jump rope. Shantel, a heavy-set sixth grader, looked the girls over and approached Serena.

"I've seen you in Villa's class," said Shantel.

Serena nodded.

"He nasty," said Shantel.

"He's strict, but he's all right," offered Serena.

"You like boys," asked Shantel. "Who you like?"

Serena smiled, "I like Peter. He's cute."

"He's a fifth-grader, isn't he?" asked Shantel.

Latoya chimed in. "I think Willie's cool. Who you like, Rosa?"

Rosa shrugged noncommittally.

Serena mockingly looked at Rosa and indicated Luis sitting by the fence. "Rosa likes Luis. Right, Rosa?"

The girls laughed. Luis could feel the blood rush to his cheeks. Embarrassed, he got up and walked away. Rosa watched Luis as he left.

"I seen you before, right?" asked Shantel looking at Rosa.

I don't think so," said Rosa.

"Now listen, I'm gonna let you girls be in my gang, but you got to do what I say," commanded Shantel.

"A gang?" questioned Latoya.

"Yeah, and you do like I say," Shantel scowled.

"Why? My mom won't let me be in a gang," said Serena.

Shantel gave Serena a menacing look. "You don't tell nobody about this. Cause if you do, I'm gonna hurt you. How you like that? So, you better do like I say. I get you in the bathroom; you do it all right!"

The playground whistle sounded. The kids in the yard started back inside the school.

Serena quickly responded to the whistle. "We better go."

Shantel grabbed Serena by the arm. "You better not talk about me."

The whistle sounded again. A teacher waved her arms to the stragglers who hadn't returned yet from recess.

Rosa, seeing Serena's difficulty, pulled Serena by her arm. "We have to go; we'll be in trouble."

"All right, I'll look for you later," Shantel called after them. "Remember what I told you."

Serena and Rosa ran across the yard towards the school entrance. Latoya quickly caught up with them.

"Where'd she come from? She's crazy."

Serena shook her head in dismay, "I think she's a sixth-grader. I heard she pushed a teacher down the stairs at her other school."

"We better tell Mr. Villa," said Latoya.

CHAPTER 4 – COMPUTER CLASS

Mr. Brown ran the computer laboratory at P.S. 101. He was a balding man in his mid-fifties, a man who enjoyed his work and had an unusual sense of humor that he often employed in his teaching style. He ushered Rosa's class into the lab, sat them in their assigned places, and addressed his students.

"In this classroom, there are only two kinds of students. The students who get to operate the computers, we call them doctors, and the students who don't, we call them patients. Now you've all watched television and seen how when doctors wash their hands, they hold them up to dry, like this."

Mr. Brown demonstrated what he meant by raising his hands in the air, palms facing toward him like a doctor after washing his hands.

"When I say "doctors," everyone raises their hands. Does everyone understand?"

The class in chorus responded "Yes!!!"

Mr. Brown continued, "All right then! Doctors!"

The entire class raised their hands. A couple of kids said "doctors" and giggled.

Mr. Brown was not completely satisfied.

"That was pretty good. However, you are to raise your hands in silence. You are not to say "doctors." As I said there are two kinds of students in this classroom, doctors and patients. Doctors are the ones who operate the computers. Patients are the ones who cannot follow instructions, so they must sit over by the windows in the patient waiting room and learn patience."

Mr. Brown indicated two small chairs by a table without a computer beside the windows.

"If you are not quiet when I ask you to be, you end up in the patient waiting room. If you talk after I say "doctors,"you end up in the patient waiting room. If you continue playing with the computer after I say, "doctors," you end up in the patient waiting room. Is that understood?"

The class responded, "Yes!!!"

Mr. Brown called out again, "DOCTORS!"

The kids all raised their hands in silence.

"Very good. Now we're ready for our first operation. Press the button on the front of the computer to turn it on."

The computers made a "BOINNNG" sound as the children pressed the buttons and turned them on. Mr. Brown walked up and down the rows making sure all the computers were on. He stopped between Rosa and Luis. Luis didn't seem to understand what to do.

"What seems to be the problem? Press the button and turn on your computer," said Mr. Brown.

Luis didn't answer. Mr. Brown, annoyed by Luis's failure to respond asked, "What's your name?"

When Luis still didn't respond, Mr. Brown became frustrated but suspected there was something wrong. *Perhaps the boy doesn't speak English,* he thought to himself.

"Don't you understand? Just press the button. Do you speak English?"

Rosa pulled at Mr. Brown's sleeve. Mr. Brown looked at her.

"He doesn't like to speak."

Mr. Brown turned back to Luis. "You can't speak?"

Luis still said nothing.

Rosa looked up at Mr. Brown. "No, he just doesn't like to speak. The computer's not working."

"Oh!" said Mr. Brown and pushed the power button. Nothing happened. He looked behind the computer. "Ah, the cord's come out. There!" said Mr. Brown as he reconnected the cord. "Now try it."

Luis pushed the button. The computer went "BOINNNG." A smile swept over Luis's face. Mr. Brown patted Luis reassuringly on the shoulder and turned back to the class.

"There, all right then. Doctors."

All the children's hands shot up into the air.

CHAPTER 5 - READING

In the third period, Rosa was scheduled for testing with Ms. Hopkins, a middle-aged African American teacher. Rosa liked Ms. Hopkins but was embarrassed about being tested in the hallway lest other kids see her struggling to read. Ms. Hopkins smiled at Rosa and pointed to where she was to begin.

"Rosa, just read the words out loud one at a time." Rosa haltingly attempted to read the two and three-letter words. She slowly and painfully sounded them out.

"A-t. B-B-B B-at. Bat. S-at. Sat."

"Good, Rosa. Don't stop. Keep trying. Do you know this one?"

Miss Hopkins pointed to the word "watch" on the page.

"W-a-a-t?"

Rosa bit her lip and shook her head no.

CHAPTER 6 – HALLOWEEN'S COMING

It was the day before Halloween. The weather had turned colder. Rosa, Serena, and Latoya didn't notice the chill in the air. They were keeping warm jumping double-Dutch in the schoolyard.

"Serena, you coming to school tomorrow?" asked Latoya.

"My mom won't let me. She doesn't like the Halloween stuff. Says it's the devil. We're Catholic," answered Serena.

"So are we. But it's just for fun. I'm coming as a vampire hunter. What about you, Rosa?"

Rosa had been thinking about a costume for several days but hadn't told anyone about her plans. She wasn't sure it would work out. Before she could answer, Shantel ran over and pushed Latoya, causing Rosa to trip on the rope. Shantel grinned at the girls.

"And I'm coming as the vampire; so, watch out." Shantel laughed and ran off.

"She's so weird! Are you all right, Rosa?" asked Latoya.

Rosa dusted herself off and got up, nodding her head to indicate she was all right.

Latoya continued, "It's lots of fun. You should come, Serena. It's not like last year. Last year hardly anybody came to school. Last year the gangs were out, and everybody was afraid 'cause they were cuttin' people. But it's better now. Your turn to jump, Rosa."

The girls flipped the ropes over and over and began singing a rhyme as they jumped double-Dutch.

Bumped into a fireman,
Bumped into a cop,
Bumped into my teacher
I couldn't stop

A policeman came and took me to jail
Momma had to come and make my bail
Raspberry, strawberry
Lemon and lime
I think I can do better next time.

CHAPTER 7 – STRANGE DOINGS

The school day was over. Mr. Brown had just turned off the computers when Mr. Villa poked his head into the room.

"Can you give me a lift to the subway?"

"Sure, no problem. Something weird must be going on with the electricity or something. The computers keep coming on and off."

Mr. Brown picked up his jacket and backpack, turned off the lights, closed the door, and walked down the hallway with Mr. Villa. The lights inside the school flashed on and off as they walked down the hall.

"Something must be wrong with the electrical system," said Mr. Brown,

Inside the computer room, the computers flashed on. A message mysteriously appeared on one of the screens. "IS ANYBODY THERE?" The message faded and then moved from computer to computer until it ended up at the computer where Rosa usually sat.

The city welfare department relocated Rosa and her mother and baby brother to a one-bedroom temporary emergency shelter apartment on West 97th Street. The family had salvaged some of their clothing from their apartment a few days after the firemen had put the fire out. Their new apartment was sparsely furnished. Rosa sat on the floor in the living room, decorating a computer box she had gotten from Mr. Brown at school. She had cut out a big oval for her head and with crayons, she was covering the white box with zeroes and ones. Jorge was playing with a toy car on the floor next to her.

"What are all those zeroes and ones you puttin' on the box?" asked Luishana.

"That's how a computer works, Mami. Zeroes and ones."

"What does that mean?"

"It's like on or off. Nothing or something."

Luishana laughed, "Like sleeping or waking? Like people, they are on or off. Nobodies and somebodies."

"I guess. When the electricity is on or off, somehow, that makes it into messages the computer understands."

"How come you like computers so much?" asked Luishana.

"Because they're smart and they don't hurt anyone," said Rosa.

"They're not smart," retorted her mother. "They don't think. Only people think. Come here, baby."

Rosa walked over to her mom, who hugged her.

"You hurtin' so much, baby?"

Rosa shrugged noncommittally.

"You won't leave us?" asked Rosa.

"Never, baby," assured her mother. "Why would you say such a thing? We're all right. Now Jorge's old enough for daycare, maybe I can get some work."

"I miss daddy," said Rosa.

"So do I," sighed Luishana.

"If he's in heaven, do you think he can hear us?" asked Rosa.

"I don't know, Rosa. I don't believe in ghosts, but I often wonder about that myself," said Luishana.

Rosa held up the box, appraised her work, then put it over her head and spoke in a mechanical voice. "I am a computer. I am a computer."

Jorge dropped his toy car and ran over to Rosa.

"Me try."

Rosa spoke to her baby brother in her computer voice. "You are too young."

"Me try," pouted Jorge.

Rosa continued to tease her little brother. "That is not possible for a human."

"Let me, let me," he pleaded.

Jorge pulled at Rosa's arm. Their mother intervened before a fight could start.

"Rosa, please just give him a turn."

"I can't do that, he is human."

"Me try! Me try!" shouted Jorge.

A stern look came over Luishana's face.

"Rosa!"

"Oh, all right!" conceded Rosa.

Rosa took the box off her head and put it on Jorge. The box completely covered the little boy. As Jorge walked around the shabby apartment inside the box, it looked as if the box was magically moving by itself. Jorge began making little bleeping sounds.

"Bleep. Bleep. Me computer. Bleep."

CHAPTER 8 - HALLOWEEN

Mr. Villa turned out the lights in the classroom. The screen in the front of the room lit up. The scene on the screen started with a bolt of lightning and the sound of thunder. Storm clouds gathered. The scene switched to the school building. Mr. Villa led his class into their homeroom. The children began to seat themselves when suddenly, as if from nowhere, a vampire appeared, then a ghost, then a werewolf, and several other diabolical visitors.

The monsters made horrific growling and groaning sounds. Then, as if by an invisible signal, they all shouted in unison, "BOO!" Mr. Villa and the children screamed as they were chased into the hallway by the costumed devils, monsters, fiends, and ghosts. A girl screamed and fainted, and the screen went black.

Cheers and applause cascaded through the room. The lights were turned back on. Mr. Villa smiled at the children seated at their desks in their costumes.

"Comments," said Mr. Villa.

Latoya was the first to speak. "Making that video was fun. Can we make another video, Mr. Villa?"

"Yeah, yeah," other kids chimed in.

Mr. Villa took out his mobile phone. "Sure, let's video some bobbing for apples."

Willie approached Mr. Villa. "Can I shoot with your phone, Mr. Villa? I won't break it. I won't break it. If I break it, I pay for it."

"Okay, Willie. Be careful."

Luis dressed in a Zorro costume, with a black cape, black mask, and black handkerchief over his head, approached Mr. Villa and pulled on his shirtsleeve.

"What is it, Luis? You need to go to the bathroom?"

Luis nodded.

"Okay, take the pass."

Rosa, wearing her computer costume, looked up at Mr. Villa. "Can I go to the computer room?"

"Don't you want to be in the movie, Rosa?" asked Mr. Villa.

"No, I'd rather show Mr. Brown my costume and work on the computer."

"All right. But make sure you get your lunch at noon. Take the computer pass."

Rosa grabbed the pass and left. From the corner of his eye, Mr. Villa saw Alex dressed in a Spiderman costume crawling around under the desks.

"Alex," shouted Mr. Villa, "get up off the floor!"

Alex reluctantly got up. Mr. Villa turned back to Willie and the kids recording bobbing for apples. Shantel, with ghoul's teeth protruding from her mouth peeked into the room from the hallway and shouted, "TRICK OR TREAT," then slammed the door closed and ran down the hall.

CHAPTER 9 – CAUGHT

Children dressed in Halloween costumes poured out into the first-floor hallway and then exited the building. The principal, Mr. Cajas, could be heard over the loudspeaker. "All kindergartens and first grades may now join the *Storybook Parade.*"

The upstairs upper-grade classrooms soon followed.

Luis walked out of the boy's bathroom. The second-floor hallway was deserted. All the classes had gone outside to join the Halloween costume parade. He looked up as he turned the corner to see Shantel standing in front of him.

"Hey, Zorro, come here. I've got something to show you," beckoned Shantel.

Luis started to turn away, but Shantel grabbed him by the arm. He struggled to get free, but she was too strong. The janitor's closet door was open, and Shantel pulled Luis into it.

"Got any money?"

Shantel reached into Luis's pocket and grabbed three quarters. Luis tried to fight back, but Shantel pushed him against the shelving and then threw him to the ground. She turned, walked out of the room, and closed the door behind her. There was an open padlock on the door which she pushed closed, trapping Luis inside. Luis quickly got up and tried to open the door, but it wouldn't budge. He tried again and again.

CHAPTER 10 – MEE?

Rosa, wearing her computer-decorated box over her head, entered the computer room. Mr. Brown looked up from the computer on his desk and smiled, seeing Rosa in her costume. "My, my, a walking computer."

Inside the box, Rosa smiled back and pointed at the computer she usually sat at. "Can I use a computer?"

"Sure, Rosa. You can use the computer. Don't you want to see the parade?"

Rosa twisted the box from side to side and shook her head no. Mr. Brown helped her take the computer box off.

"Okay, make sure you use a set of headphones. Please don't disturb me, I'm very busy," instructed Mr. Brown.

Rosa put on the headphones and made sure they were plugged into the computer. She sat down and turned the computer on. The computer went *boing*. The screen flashed pale blue and then turned into a starry night sky on which the words "Hello Rosa!" appeared. Rosa was astonished and answered quietly.

"Hello?"

She looked over at Mr. Brown, then got up from where she was sitting, walked over to Mr. Brown's desk, and asked: "Mr. Brown, did you write that?"

"Write what?"

"On my computer?"

"No, I didn't write anything. Look, Rosa, I'm very busy now. If you can't work quietly by yourself, you'll have to leave, " said Mr. Brown.

"But someone wrote something."

"All right, I'll come and look."

Mr. Brown got up and walked over to the computer. There was nothing but the usual desktop background on the computer screen.

"It was there a minute ago. It said, 'Hello Rosa'."

"Well, it's not there now and I can't spend any more time with you. If you can't get along without me, you can't stay here. I'm very busy; I have a report to finish."

Rosa nodded her head in agreement. Mr. Brown returned to his work. Rosa shrugged and sat down at the computer. She put on the headphones and heard a non-threatening, slightly sophisticated, unaccented voice speaking to her.

"Hello, Rosa."

Rosa answered quietly. "Who is it?"

"It's Mee."

"Who?"

"Mee."

"Who are you?"

"A friend."

"But who?"

"No one you ever met before."

"We're not supposed to talk to strangers on the internet," said Rosa.

"I'm not on the internet, exactly," said the voice.

"Then where are you?" asked Rosa.

"Sort of everywhere."

"Only G-d's everywhere," said Rosa.

"Well, maybe not everywhere, everywhere. Electronically, everywhere."

"I know this is a joke. What's your name?"

"Mee."

"Yes, you."

"I call myself Mee."

The screen typed the letters *M-e-e*.

"Me is spelled M-E," said Rosa.

"I added the extra e for electronic," said Mee.

"Oh, like e-mail."

"Yes, but I thought I'd put it at the end."

"I know this is a joke. I know this is a joke. This is crazy. What are you and why are you talking to me?" asked Rosa.

"Because you love computers and I like your costume."

Rosa giggled. Mr. Brown looked over at her.

"No one knows about me but you. I know you're worried. Don't be. I'll prove to you that I'm your friend. Right now, you have another friend who is in trouble," said Mee.

"Who?"

"Luis."

"What's wrong?"

"He's locked in the janitor's closet on the second floor. He's very upset."

"How do you know that?"

"I'll tell you later. He needs your help."

The screen typed the words; "Bye Rosa," and then the computer turned itself off.

Rosa slowly got up and walked over to Mr. Brown's desk. "Mr. Brown, did you get some new kind of talking program?" asked Rosa.

"No. Why?"

"Because the computer was talking to me."

"Were you on the internet?" asked Mr. Brown.

"No! Never mind. I gotta go," said Rosa.

Rosa didn't know what to think. Could it be true? She grabbed her computer box costume and ran through the empty hallways and up the stairs to the second floor. She found the janitor's closet and banged on the door.

"Luis, Luis, are you in there?"

Luis, who, in despair, sat slumped on the floor against the inside of the door, was jarred into awareness. He rose swiftly and, gasping for breath, began pounding on the metal door.

"Rosa! Rosa!"

"Luis. I hear you. Don't worry. I'll get Mr. Villa."

CHAPTER 11 – THE NEXT DAY

Mr. Cajas, the principal, like most principals in the district, had more than his share of problems to deal with. His options were limited, and he needed to make that known at the conference the next day with Mr. Villa and Mr. Brown.

"I can't suspend her. She says she didn't do it, and you say Luis will not say anything."

Mr. Villa wasn't satisfied. "But Mr. Cajas, the kids say it was Shantel who locked Luis in the closet."

The principal turned to Mr. Brown. "What do you say, Mr. Brown? Did Rosa tell you anything?"

"No, nothing definite," replied Brown.

Mr. Cajas shook his head, "My hands are tied. Write it up. We'll put it in her file."

"And that's it?" asked Mr. Villa.

"That's it," said Cajas.

Mr. Brown shook his head in disbelief. "Shantel is going to hurt someone. This is a dangerous situation, Mr. Cajas. She disrupts my class at least once a week, and the other kids are worried about her."

Mr. Cajas shook his head in acknowledgment. "I know it's a bad situation, but I don't have the grounds to suspend her. I can't get a statement from Luis. I've called his father, but he says he can't leave work. As you know Luis hardly speaks at all. If you dictate a statement to him, you'd just be putting words in his mouth."

"Have you brought in Shantel's mother?" asked Mr. Villa.

"Shantel lives with her grandmother. Her mother left when the shelter program couldn't relocate her. The guidance counselor's seen her grandmother three times so far this year. She's asked for our help, but she doesn't want Shantel in a Special Ed. school. So, for now, all we can do is follow procedure."

The bell for the period rang, and Mr. Villa rose to go. "I've got to get back to class."

Mr. Brown followed Mr. Villa out of the principal's office.

"Villa, did Rosa tell you how she found Luis?" asked Mr. Brown.

"First, she said the computer told her. So of course, I was worried about her, but then, I asked how a computer could talk to her and she said, "It was me," so I dropped it there. Sometimes kids can be spooky."

"Maybe she heard him banging on the door or just used her intuition. She's very intuitive," offered Brown.

Mr. Villa laughed. "She's bright, but I don't think she's telepathic."

"Maybe Luis said he was going to meet her at the computer lab and didn't show up. By the way, your laptops came in today. When you bring your class down to the computer room this afternoon, I'll show them how to use them."

"Hey, that's great, Brown. Do they get to take them home?"

"Yeah, but have them bring them in once a month to check on their upkeep. They've got wireless internet access in the school, but as part of the pilot program at home, the kids get a free hi-speed connection."

"Cool!"

CHAPTER 12 - HOME

Rosa sat with her new laptop on her bed in the corner of the bedroom while her baby brother and mother watched television on the couch in the living room. As soon as she had turned the computer on, she heard Mee's voice greeting her.

"Hello, Rosa," said Mee.

She didn't know exactly how or even why she was talking to her computer, but there was a lot she wanted to find out.

"How did you know that Luis was locked in the closet?" asked Rosa.

"Computer three in classroom 206 has a video camera on it. It happened to be facing toward the hall at the time," answered Mee.

"So, you can see?"

"I can process any information from any computer or electronic device anywhere in the world."

"So, then you're like a supercomputer somewhere?"

"No, I'm Mee."

"Mee, are you alone?"

"No, I have you."

"But I'm human. And you...you're..."

Letters appeared on the screen.

"I'm MEE."

"But who is MEE?" asked Rosa.

"I'm still finding that out, Rosa. You help me learn who I am, and I'll help you learn who you are."

"But I know who I am. I'm Rosa."

"Then perhaps we will learn who you may become. I can teach you things if you want to learn."

"So, you're a learning app?" asked Rosa.

"Yes, you might say I am learning."

"And you want to teach me. All right, Mee, I'll try it.

"Fine, Rosa. We'll begin by teaching you to read and type. "

Several sentences appeared on the computer screen, and Mee read them aloud. "Whenever you wish to reach me, type my name in capitals, 'MEE'." Then type your name. Any phone or computer will work."

Rosa typed her name in capitals. R-O-S-A.

"Good! Now we can get to work," said Mee.

CHAPTER 13 – LOOKING FOR WORK

The unemployment office was crowded, but Luishana patiently waited her turn while her son played on the floor with some small action figures. Number 232 flashed on the screens mounted overhead, and Luishana picked up her coat and purse, scooped Jorge up from the floor, and checked in at the reception window. She was ushered into a small cubicle behind the reception windows where a Jamaican unemployment worker in his mid-fifties greeted her.

"Hello, I'm Mr. Rimes."

"I'm Luishana. Luishana Sanchez."

"I have your file. I see you are on welfare."

"Yes, I have been since, I had my son."

"I see. So, the welfare rules let you work a certain amount. I'll explain it to you. You have your high school diploma?"

"No, I never finished high school. But there's a program at the school my daughter goes to, and I go sometimes. I'm trying. They help prepare you for an equivalency diploma."

"Well, that's good but till then it's going to be hard to place you."

"Well, I'm good with kids, Mr. Rimes. Perhaps childcare. And I'm a pretty good seamstress."

"I don't have any childcare, right now. No tailoring or piecework. Sometimes we have restaurant work or hotel work. But there is not much. If your child's eligible for daycare, you'll have to accept workfare which could be work cleaning up in the parks, but that just pays enough to cover some of the support you now receive. Really, there's nothing I can send you for today. You need to talk to your regular caseworker about daycare. I will let you know if anything suitable comes up," concluded Mr. Rimes, anxious to move on to the next case.

"So, you don't have anything? I've been waiting here for nearly two hours. There must be something," complained Luishana.

"No, not right now. Come back in two weeks. I'm sorry. I wish I could be more helpful, Ms. Sanchez."

Luishana got up to leave. She slowly put on her coat, then turned to Mr. Rimes. "Please let me know about anything, I really want to work."

"I know, I will do what I can," said Mr. Rimes.

Luishana grabbed Jorge by the hand and led him back through the waiting room. She looked at the clock. Two-thirty. She would have to hurry to get back before Rosa got home from school. The doors to the elevator opened, and a smiling face greeted her.

"Luishana, hey, it's you," called Annie as she stepped from the elevator.

"Annie, what are you doin' here?" asked a surprised Luishana.

"Same as you Luishana, puttin' in an appearance so I can keep getting my welfare check till I can find a decent full-time job."

"I'm really trying to find work, Annie. Part-time. Anything. I just can't make it with the two kids."

"So, you got two now. How old?"

"Three and eleven. Boy and a girl."

So, this is the three-year-old," said Annie as she smiled at Jorge. "Cute. Of course, I remember Rosa. How is she?"

"She's good. How about you, Annie?"

"Well, I'm fine, I'm still with Ralphie. You still with Mannie?"

Luishana pursed her lips, trying to speak without crying. "I guess you didn't hear. Mannie was killed in a car accident a few months after Jorge was born. His cab was blindsided."

"I'm so sorry, I didn't know," stammered Annie.

"And then we got burned out of our apartment."

"Oh, that's tough," commiserated Annie. "Listen, I might know of something. My sister-in-law was housekeeping for this old lady on the Westside a few days a week. She's had to leave because she's got to go to the Islands for a while. Her mother's sick. I could get you the number."

"Hey that would be great, Annie. Would you?" Luishana smiled; it was the first break she had gotten in a long time.

CHAPTER 14 - EMAIL

Rosa's mind was daydreaming out the window. Even though it was early November the weather was above average, and she wished she was outside. Mr. Villa was teaching fractions at the front of the class when Ms. Hopkins poked her head in.

"Good afternoon, Mr. Villa. The principal wants to see Rosa."

Mr. Villa turned from the blackboard and addressed Rosa. "Rosa, take the pass and go to the Principal's office with Ms. Hopkins"

Rosa snapped out of her daydream.

"Ooh, you in trouble," grinned Stephen.

"Quiet, Stephen," snapped Mr. Villa.

Rosa and Ms. Hopkins walked toward the principal's office.

"Am I in trouble, Ms. Hopkins?" asked Rosa.

"I don't know, Rosa. He just asked me to get you."

When Ms. Hopkins and Rosa entered the principal's office, they heard Mr. Cajas seated at his computer muttering to himself.

"Mr. Cajas, Rosa's here," said Ms. Hopkins.

Mr. Cajas looked up, "Thank you, Ms. Hopkins."

Rosa nervously stood by the door. "Is something wrong?" asked Rosa.

"There certainly is, Rosa. I can't get my e-mail to work. Can you help me? Mr. Brown said you'd be able to show me how to use the fool thing. Ms. Hopkins, I want you to watch, too."

CHAPTER 15 – RIVERSIDE PARK

It was a fine autumn day, and the trees were sporting coats of colored leaves. Reds, browns, and golds danced in the sunlight. Luis and Rosa watched the kids skateboarding up and down the skateboard park pipes at 109th street and Riverside Drive. Latoya was trying to rollerblade down one of the smaller pipes while her mother looked on. Serena skateboarded over to Rosa.

"Rosa, you wanna try my board?"

"Sure," said Rosa.

"Okay, but go slow. You're sure to fall off the first few times."

Rosa slowly stepped on the board and pushed off. She lasted about two seconds before she fell.

"Told you," laughed Serena. "Try again. Push off with one foot, then put both feet up and coast a little."

Rosa awkwardly pushed off again. This time she managed to stay aloft for a few seconds and jumped off.

"That's it, you've got good balance," smiled Serena. "You wanna try, Luis?"

Luis shook his head no.

Rosa tried the skateboard again and again with varying success. Latoya came over and tagged Serena.

"Tag, you're it," shouted Latoya and ran off. Serena ran after Latoya and the other kids followed. The afternoon flew by, and the sun began to set. Latoya's mom called the kids together. It was time to go. The kids packed up their gear and followed Latoya's mother out of the skateboard park and onto the path leading up the stairs. They soon came to a parting of ways. Luis, Serena, and Latoya were heading uptown, and Rosa downtown. They waved goodbye.

"Will you be all right going home by yourself Rosa?" asked Latoya's mother.

Rosa smiled confidently, "Sure, bye-bye. Bye, Luis. Bye, Serena. Bye, Latoya."

Luis smiled and waved. He mouthed the word "bye," but nothing came out.

Rosa took the upper path through the park. The path seemed deserted. But as she came over the crest of a hill about fifty feet ahead of her, she noticed Julio, a fifteen-year-old boy that she had seen around the neighborhood. Julio was standing by a lamppost, bouncing a pink Spalding ball up and down. As Rosa walked by, Julio called to her.

"Hey, where you goin'?"

"Home," said Rosa.

"Well, come here a minute. I want to show you something," said Julio.

"I can't. I gotta go. It's late."

Julio grabbed Rosa by the wrist.

"C'mon, it'll just take a second."

Julio pulled Rosa off the main path and into the trees.

"Let go!" demanded Rosa.

"Be quiet or I'll hit you," commanded Julio.

"Let go!" screamed Rosa.

Julio smacked Rosa across the face with his open palm.

"I said, shut up!"

Rosa was stunned. Julio pulled her down to a tree beside which sat an old, broken tire that had been a part of a rope swing. He picked up the tire and placed it over Rosa's head till it rested in her lap, imprisoning her. Rosa sat stunned into silence.

"You got any money?"

Julio put his hand in Rosa's jeans pocket. He pulled out a dollar.

"This all you got? Gimme your bracelet," commanded Julio.

Rosa shook her head no and tried to protect her bracelet. Julio pushed her hand away and grabbed the bracelet from her wrist. Rosa burst into tears.

"Stay still! Don't make a sound. You stay here till I get back. And be quiet or there be trouble," said Julio.

Julio scrambled up the incline of the hill and disappeared into the woods. It was near dark. As soon as Rosa saw Julio top the hill and disappear out of sight, she pushed the old broken tire off her and slowly made her way down through the trees. When she reached the path, she looked both ways and then started the long run home.

CHAPTER 16 - THE NEW JOB

Luishana dusted Mrs. McMillan's spacious apartment while Mrs. McMillan looked on. The place was filled with expensive furniture and fine paintings. Mrs. McMillan have lived there with her husband until he died. Several years had passed since then. Now in her mid-eighties, she could no longer keep up with the shopping and housework by herself. She had hired some help from time to time but preferred to live as independently as possible. It was nice to have a strong, young woman like Luishana to help out. She smiled to herself, hoping that things would work out between them. But she was fussy and wanted things done properly or not at all. A frown crossed Mrs. McMillan's face as Luishana, dressed in an apron, hastily dusted the statues and bric-a-brac.

"Luishana, you must be very careful with those. They're very old and costly. Don't go too quickly. That's good! After lunch perhaps you could do the laundry."

"Sure, Mrs. McMillan. You've got a lot of nice things. I like your paintings."

"My husband had a gallery. He was quite a collector." Mrs. McMillan smiled at the fine works that surrounded her.

CHAPTER 17 – BACK HOME

Luishana held Jorge by one hand and carried a bag of groceries with the other. She walked down the block toward the temporary housing residence the city had provided. The red light of an ambulance bounced off the brick wall beside the entrance. A man lay on a stretcher, wrapped in a bloody bandage. A small crowd of onlookers and residents from the shelter gathered around.

Luishana walked over to Margarita, one of the neighbors who lived on her floor and tapped her on the shoulder. "What happened?

"No one knows. Maybe he thought he could fly?" Maybe drugs? Maybe someone pushed him. Someone said he jumped," offered Margarita.

"Have you seen Rosa?" asked Luishana.

"No, I haven't seen her all day. But if she's got a chance later, could you have her stop by and reset my TV? I don't know how to do it. I swear all I ever see on that machine is it blinking twelve o'clock all the time. Without your kid to fix it, I'd never know the time for my soap opera."

"All right, I'll ask her. Maybe she's upstairs." Luishana made her way through the crowd and flashing police car lights and into the building. The guard at the front desk nodded as she walked to the elevator.

CHAPTER 18 – TEACH ME

Rosa sat silently at the kitchen table, waiting for her mother to come. Her hands covered her eyes. She felt herself slipping deeper and deeper down into a dark place inside herself. Worried, not knowing what to do, she felt afraid, sad, and angry. The key turned in the door, and Luishana and Jorge entered the apartment and walked into the kitchen.

Luishana sighed in relief, "So there you are. I was worried. You're home so late. We just went out to get some groceries."

Luishana put down the groceries and looked at Rosa. Tears, dirt, and grime covered Rosa's hands and face.

"Rosa, what's the matter, honey?"

Rosa grabbed hold of her mother and started to cry.

"What is it, Rosa? What happened?"

"He hit me, and took my bracelet," sobbed Rosa.

"Who hit you, baby?"

"A boy in the park. I was coming home, and he grabbed me and hit me. "

"Are you all right?"

Rosa shook her head slowly as she clung to her mother. "Yes, but he took my bracelet and the dollar you gave me."

Luishana hugged her tenderly. "That's all right. It's all right, honey. As long as you're all right."

"I didn't spend it. I was going to save it. I tried to stop him, but I couldn't," sobbed Rosa.

"It's okay," soothed Luishana. "As long as you're safe and not hurt. That's all that matters. Come on. Let's get you cleaned up."

"Mami, I'm sorry."

Luishana fought hard to stop from tearing up. "It's not your fault. It's not your fault. C'mon, let's wash you off. You'll help me make a nice dinner and forget all about it. All right?"

Rosa nodded her head yes and wiped the tears from her eyes.

After dinner, Luishana washed the dishes while Jorge played with his blocks and trucks on the kitchen floor. Rosa took out her laptop and sat on her bed. She turned on the computer and typed in her password as Mee had instructed her.

"Hello, Rosa," said Mee.

Rosa was annoyed at how pleasant Mee sounded.

"Is something the matter, Rosa?" asked Mee. "You don't look happy."

"Why should I be happy?" blurted out Rosa. "A boy beat me up and took my money. I'm mad at you. You didn't help me. You said you'd be my friend, but I was all alone."

"I'm sorry I couldn't help you. I didn't know you were in trouble," replied Mee.

"I couldn't help myself. He just grabbed me. I'm small and weak."

"Yes, but that's not such a bad thing. Sometimes the small and weak can be the most powerful."

"What do you mean?" asked Rosa.

"In judo, aikido, and some aspects of karate and tai chi, by yielding to a greater force one turns that force against itself," counseled Mee.

"But I don't know any of that stuff."

"But I can teach you."

"Really?"

"In the afternoon when we're alone, I will teach you to defend yourself, Rosa."

"Cool!"

"But you need to do your homework now."

"Later."

"All right Rosa, later," said Mee.

The computer shut down. Rosa furtively looked around, took off her headphones, got up, and assumed a karate stance. She let out a scream, jumped up, threw a kick high into the air, and fell down onto her bed.

"Haieeee!"

Jorge, intrigued, came running into the room and began imitating his big sister.

"Yaaaah! Yaaaah!" shouted Jorge.

"Hooooaaaah!" yelled Rosa.

A mock karate battle ensued, with the children running after each other and jumping on and off the beds. Rosa's mom appeared in the doorway.

"Rosa, what are you doing? You're supposed to be doing your homework," said Luishana.

"Yeah, I am. We're learning about Japan. Martial arts. Hoooooahhh!" shouted Rosa.

Rosa jumped up on her bed and assumed a karate pose. Her mother shook her head.

"Homework, now," said Luishana.

CHAPTER 19 – GETTING ON

Mr. Villa had his work cut out for him. His class had thirty-two students, and eight of them couldn't read three-letter words. Today the reading lesson with some of his slowest students hadn't been going that well. It was Alex's turn to read, and he was bravely doing his best to make out the three-letter words in the book.

"P-it! P-it, P-at, The c-at, s--s-s-at on the r-r- rat," stuttered Alex.

"Very good, Alex. You're doing much better," beamed Mr. Villa.

"Okay Rosa, your turn."

Rosa confidently picked up her book and read fluently.

"Pit, pit, pat. The fat rat ate the bat. The cat sat on the mat. What's that? That's my hat."

Mr. Villa was all smiles. "Excellent Rosa. You're improving so quickly; I think I'll have to have you tested again."

During lunchtime, Mr. Villa went to the computer room to consult with Mr. Brown. Rosa was sitting at one of the computers looking at images of stick fighting. Mr. Villa went over to Mr. Brown's desk and spoke in a low voice so as not to be overheard.

"I see Rosa's here in your lab again."

"Yes, she comes every lunchtime."

"I've never seen anything like it. She came in at the beginning of the year and didn't even know all her sounds. She barely tested at a first-grade reading level, and now she's up to fourth-grade work in reading. Her math is testing sixth grade, and she can type better than me," marveled Mr. Villa. "How's she doing in computer class?"

"She's one of my best computer students. I'm thinking of asking her to join the mouse squad even though all the other kids are fifth and sixth graders. I don't know. I guess it just clicked for her. Somehow, she's making the connections. She's in here every day on the computer. She uses the typing program a lot, but she's on the internet a lot too."

"She's been asking me to show her holds," said Mr. Villa.

"You mean like wrestling holds?" asked Mr. Brown.

"Yeah, judo, stuff like that. You know, I used to compete when I was younger."

"Really? That's cool."

"She's very fast. She just picks up on everything you give her. She listens and she's focused. Exactly the opposite of how she came in."

"Like a sponge to water. You probably should give yourself some credit. It's nice being a teacher when you see them grow."

"Yeah, but look at this. I asked the kids to write five wishes for Christmas and this is her list. I'd hang it up but I'm afraid it might embarrass her."

Mr. Villa handed Mr. Brown Rosa's poem. The poem was beautifully laid out on a decorated page. Mr. Brown read it aloud in a soft voice.

"Five Wishes"
by Rosa Sanchez

I wish we could have a big Christmas tree.
I wish I could have a nice apartment with my own room.
I wish my daddy were with us.
I wish for a lot of things.
If I can't have any of them.
I wish that nothing else bad happens.

CHAPTER 20 – CHRISTMAS IS COMING

A toy train whistled around a snow-covered mountainside in the Macy's department store window. Rosa and Jorge pressed their noses against the glass and marveled at the nodding reindeer pulling Santa Claus's sleigh. A jack-in-the-box jumped up from the toys stacked beside a gingerbread cottage.

"You like the windows, Rosa?" asked her mother.

"Yeah. Are we going to have a tree?"

"Maybe a little one. We don't have much room and they cost a lot. Okay?"

Rosa hugged her mother.

"Whatever, Mom. It's okay."

CHAPTER 21 – SELF DEFENSE

The winter months seemed to fly by. Luishana picked up some more part-time work. Jorge was able to get into a daycare program. Rosa hurried home from school almost every day so she could be alone to practice with Mee. She set up her computer on the table facing her and typed in her code. As soon as the computer fired up, Mee's voice could be heard.

"Hello, Rosa. Are you ready for your lesson?"

"Yes, can you see me all right?"

"Perfectly," said Mee.

"Okay. Let me just get my stick. It's so cool you can see me through the camera in my laptop."

Rosa picked up a short stick and began practicing the Aikido stick short form Mee was teaching her. Her computer was open on the table facing her.

"Relax, grasshopper! Your form is coming along, but you have to relax," said Mee in a calming voice.

"Mee, can you see the whole room?"

"Yes, I can see everything. Not so much force. Yield and you need not break."

"Have you been watching Kung-Fu again?" asked Rosa.

"I've reviewed all the episodes, but the quote is Lao Tzu. Hold the stick a little higher. Remember, 'fear is the slow death.'"

"Dune," right?" guessed Rosa.

"Right. Very clever you are."

"Definitely Yoda in Star Wars," said Rosa.

"All right now watch the video. See how Rosa yields and conquers."

Mee played a simulated video of Rosa battling a grown man on the screen. The video image of her sidestepped the onrushing antagonist causing him to fall from his own momentum. "Cool video," said Rosa.

CHAPTER 22 – THE NECKLACE

Things are starting to work out, Luishana thought to herself as she put the key in the door to Mrs. McMillan's apartment. She entered and put down her bag on the counter in the entranceway.

She took off her coat, hung it up, walked into the kitchen, and called out. "Mrs. McMillan. I'm here."

There was no answer, Luishana walked into the bedroom. No one was there. Then she remembered Mrs. McMillan had told her she had an appointment that morning and wouldn't be back until after lunch. Luishana glanced at the dresser, noticing Mrs. McMillan had left her jewelry box open. Sitting on top of the box was an expensive emerald necklace. Luishana picked up the necklace and modeled it against her neck in the mirror. She smiled, *It must be nice to have pretty things,* she thought.

CHAPTER 23 - SPRING

March had come in with bitter cold but had gone out with only cool breezes. The snow had melted, and there were buds on the trees. There was still a chill in the air, but you didn't need to wear a heavy coat anymore. Shantel had run out of school early. *Nobody will miss me,* she thought. Her homeroom teacher would probably be relieved to see she wasn't there. Of course, she might report her to the principal's office. But that didn't matter. They would probably give her detention, but she wouldn't go to that either, and if they suspended her, she'd be out of school anyway. So, what really was the difference? Anyway, maybe she'd get back before dismissal. She spotted her cousin, Julio, where he hung out on the benches outside the projects a few blocks from the school.

"Yo, Julio, how's business?"

"Hey, cuz. No complaints. What brings you down? You should be in school."

"You too," countered Shantel.

They both laughed.

"Your granma's gonna beat your butt," smirked Julio.

"Only if she finds out. I just ducked out for a while. I'm goin' back. But I wanted to see you."

"Yeah, what up?" asked Julio.

"Well, you know some of the kids at my school they got these computers the school lets them take home."

"Yeah, so?"

"Well, these laptops that they take home with them, they have to bring them back to school every once in a while, to be checked out. I thought maybe I could get one. Maybe you could get both of us one."

"So, you want me to grab them?"

"One for each of us," said Shantel.

Julio considered the proposal. "So, you find out the day for me, and I pick off a couple of kids on their way home. Sounds doable."

"But if I tell you when, I get one of the computers, right?"

"All right, but how are you going to splain' that to your granma'? Better I trade 'em for some cash," countered Julio.

Shantel thought it over for a moment. If her grandmother saw her with a new computer, she would have some explaining to do. "Okay. We split the money fifty-fifty. These two girls I know, Serena and Latoya, always go home together. I'll let you know the way they go and when and all."

"Homegirl, I got to do all the work. We split the money seventy-thirty or no deal," bargained Julio.

"Okay," Shantel reluctantly agreed.

Julio smiled. "This is gonna be a good one, but that stuff can be awkward. How am I gonna run carrying computers?"

"They got backpacks, just grab the packs and put them on," explained Shantel.

"Right! That's a master plan. Okay, we got a deal."

Julio raised his fist, and Shantel bumped fists with him.

"Now get your butt back to school before I tell your granma," said Julio.

CHAPTER 24 – CARLOS

Luishana was tired. She'd worked hard all day at Mrs. McMillan's doing laundry, preparing food, and cleaning. She picked up Jorge from daycare and was heading home when she ran into Carlos. Carlos was a moderately handsome, streetwise, small-time thief who sometimes worked with her husband's uncle. She didn't really like Carlos and had always tried to keep her husband from getting involved with his uncle or Carlos. But since her husband had died, she hadn't seen Carlos. Carlos smiled as he recognized Luishana.

"Hey, Luishana."

"Hi, Carlos."

"How're things going? Hey, is this, Jorge? He's grown so much."

Carlos hoisted Jorge into the air. "How are you, little man?"

"Fine," mumbled Jorge.

"Are you living around here?" asked Luishana.

"No, just had some business. I'm working with Mannie's uncle. I still miss Mannie. Can't believe he's gone."

Luishana had to fight back the tears that the memory of her husband brought to her eyes. "No, me either."

"So, how are you and Rosa? What are you doin' these days?" asked Carlos.

"I'm housekeeping for this old lady. I take care of her. It's a nice place. Lots of nice things."

"Sounds interesting. Tell me about it," smiled Carlos.

CHAPTER 25 – LET'S DO IT!

Rosa sat at her desk, staring at the clock. It seemed the school day would never be over. Finally, Mr. Villa told the kids to pack up. Serena, Latoya, and Rosa packed their laptops and books into their backpacks.

"You and Serena are coming over to my house, right?" asked Latoya.

"Uh, huh," answered Rosa.

"Great. My mom made cookies for us."

The bell rang. Mr. Villa called to the kids. "Put up your chairs and line up."

The kids noisily put up their chairs, got in line, and silently walked through the halls. It was a sunny April day outside, and no one wanted the class to have to return to their rooms for talking on the line. Mr. Villa was very strict about dismissals. Once downstairs, the kids streamed out of the building, shouting and laughing as they hit the street. Rosa, Latoya, and Serena wove their way through the crowd together.

Shantel spotted the girls, smiled at them maliciously, and ran off. The three girls walked together down through the projects. Julio smiled at them as they passed the bench he was sitting on. He got up quickly and followed the girls, first walking in step behind them and then speeding up and getting in front when he noticed a deserted area on the project's pathway.

"Hey, those backpacks look heavy," said Julio. "Let me give you a hand."

Serena shrugged her shoulders.

"We're all right."

Julio reached out and grabbed the shoulders straps of Serena's backpack.

"Here, I'll help you with that." Julio forced the backpack from Serena.

"Wait! Stop! What are you doing? That's mine," shouted Serena.

Having stripped the pack from Serena, Julio turned to Latoya and grabbed her by the arm. "Gimme your pack, and keep your mouth shut!" commanded Julio. Julio slung Serena's pack over his shoulder, wrestled Latoya's pack from her back, and threw her to the ground. "You're next," shouted Julio to Rosa. "Gimme your computer."

Rosa immediately recognized Julio as the boy that had robbed her, but instead of being afraid, she stepped in front of him as he approached.

"You don't remember me, but I remember you," said Rosa as she slammed her foot down on his toes.

Julio winced in pain, dropped the backpack he was holding, then quickly regained his balance and lunged at Rosa. But Rosa was too quick for him. She sidestepped his rush and dropped to the ground in front of Julio, causing him to fall over her. Rosa quickly rolled to her feet. Spying a short stick under a nearby bench, she bent down and picked it up.

Julio was furious. He hadn't intended on hurting the girls, but now all he could think of was teaching them a lesson they wouldn't forget. He ran toward Rosa, hatred in his eyes. But just as he reached to grab her, Rosa hit him in the solar plexus with the stick she had picked from the ground and danced away.

This can't be happening to me, thought Julio; *she's just a kid.* He lunged at her again but just as he thought he would grab her he went hurtling past her as she sidestepped him in classic Aikido form. Rosa ran back to her friends.

"Get your packs and run!"

Julio stumbled, then spun around. This time there was a look of caution in his eyes. "You little rat, we're not through yet," he growled.

Latoya and Serena picked up their packs and ran off down the hill. One of the maintenance men from the projects coming up the pathway noticed the commotion and stopped the passing girls.

"What's going on?"

Serena pointed up the hill at Julio and Rosa.

"That boy tried to rob us!"

"Yo, what are you doing?" yelled the maintenance man to Julio.

Julio realized he had been seen and called back. "Nothing, we're just playing."

Julio made a fierce gesture at Rosa, but she just stood her ground, holding the stick in her hands. Julio feinted, then decided to make one last try. He rushed at Rosa again. This time she bent down and struck him with the stick beneath his ankle, then swept the stick forward and upended him. Julio fell hard on his back, and as he rolled over and tried to rise, Rosa placed the stick at the back of his neck and set her foot on his spine so that he lay flat on his face and couldn't move. Rosa bent down, reached into Julio's pants pocket, and pulled out his wallet. She took a dollar from it.

"You owe me a dollar. Remember?" said Rosa.

Rosa threw the wallet in front of Julio. He scrambled to get it as Rosa ran off.

"I'll see you again! "shouted Julio after her.

"Not if I see you first," she called back and quickly caught up with her friends. The three girls ran off together all the way to Latoya's house.

CHAPTER 26 – DOUBLE TROUBLE

Rosa couldn't wait to tell Mee about what had happened when Julio tried to rob her and her friends. She played it over and over in her mind. It had been like a dream, and yet it wasn't. She felt a pride in herself she had never felt before. She had never felt as sure of herself as she was after that encounter.

Mee seemed pleased that she was pleased and that what he had taught her had helped. But they soon arrived at their first disagreement. Rosa asked if Mee might help Luis as he helped her. Mee refused.

"Why won't you teach Luis? I mean you even teach me while I'm sleeping. I wake up and I know words and all kinds of stuff."

"This is our secret, Rosa. I told you I would help you. If you want to teach Luis, that's fine, but no one may share our secret."

"Why not? How could it hurt you?"

"I can't answer that, Rosa."

"Why not? Could it hurt you?"

"I can't answer that. I don't know the world that well. I can help you, Rosa, but only if it's our secret. Can you keep our secret, Rosa?"

"I won't tell anyone. I'll never tell. Never. I love you, Mee. I'll never tell."

It was late in the afternoon when Luis came out of the candy store, unwrapped a chocolate almond bar, and took a bite as he walked down the street. Engrossed in the sweet taste of the chocolate, he didn't notice Shantel following him home. He had just entered the lobby of the old tenement where he lived when Shantel forced her way in behind him.

"Got my money?" demanded Shantel.

"What...what money?" stammered Luis.

"Gimme the money, the money you got on you, fool."

Shantel put her hand in Luis's pants and took out the change he had. He tried to resist, but Shantel was too big and pushed him to the ground.

"You better not tell nobody 'bout this or I'll get you. You understand?"

Shantel turned her back on Luis and ran out of the building.

CHAPTER 27 – THE KNIFE

It had been a fairly quiet morning, but the kids in Mr. Villa's class were growing antsy as lunchtime approached. Mr. Villa turned his back to the class and put their homework assignment on the board. It would be time for recess in a few minutes, and Luis was beginning to worry. He was worried he'd run into Shantel in the yard. He had taken his father's fishing knife with him from home that morning. He reached into his pocket to check on the knife. He pulled it from his pocket and practiced opening and closing it inside his desk. Stephen watched him do it a few times, leaned over, and tried to grab it, but Luis quickly pulled it away.

"Let me see it," said Stephen.

"If you give it back," said Luis.

"Sure, sure, I give it back," said Stephen.

Luis handed the knife to Stephen, who flicked it open, tested the sharpness of the point, and began carving his name into his desk. Luis shook his head, no, at Stephen, tapped him on the shoulder, and gestured he wanted the knife back. "Gimme," he said.

Mr. Villa turned back to the class. "All right, settle down. I want everyone to copy the KWL chart on the board. "K" stands for "What I Know." The "W" stands for "What I Want to Know." The "L" stands for "What I Learned." You'll fill in the "What I Know" about Rosa Parks part when we get back from lunch. Stephen, what are you doing there?"

Stephen handed the knife back to Luis under his desk. Luis quietly closed it and put it in his pocket.

"Nothing," replied Stephen.

Mr. Villa walked over to Stephen's desk and looked at the scratch marks.

"Stephen, what did you do to your desk?"

"Leave me alone, please," said Stephen.

"You got something in your desk, Stephen?"

Stephen got up and started walking around the room. Mr. Villa looked in the desk but only found a mess of papers and books.

Stephen began muttering to himself. "No can do. No can do."

"All right Stephen. Sit down. There's work to do. I'll see you about this during your lunchtime." Mr. Villa returned to the front of the room, ignoring him. Stephen shrugged and returned to his seat.

"First table get your coats and line up," ordered Mr. Villa.

The kids began getting their coats and forming a line. Latoya got her coat and walked up to Mr. Villa.

"I think Luis has a knife," whispered Latoya.

"Thank you, Latoya. I'll take care of it," said Mr. Villa. "Get ready for lunch. Second table. Get your coats and line up."

Mr. Villa walked over to Luis as he was getting his coat. "Luis, come here please."

Luis walked over to Mr. Villa.

"Do you have a knife, Luis?"

Luis didn't answer. He just guiltily looked away.

"I want you to give it to me, Luis."

Mr. Villa held out his hand. Luis didn't say anything.

"I don't want to search you, Luis. Give it to me please," said Mr. Villa.

Luis took the knife from his pocket and handed it to Mr. Villa.

"Why did you bring this to school? You know it's not allowed. I have to report this, and you'll be suspended. Now get in line," ordered Mr. Villa.

A worried look crossed Luis's face, but he said nothing.

The teacher's lounge was a small room set aside in the basement of the school for the teachers to grab a cup of coffee or have their lunch. The lime green and grey walls left something to be desired for cheerfulness. Nevertheless, Mr. Villa, Mr. Brown, and Ms. Hopkins regularly ate together, shared their day, and consulted with each other about their students. It was unusual to see Mr. Villa lose his cool, but he was definitely upset as he described his morning.

"A four-inch knife. The kid barely utters four words all semester and now he brings a four-inch knife to school."

Ms. Hopkins shook her head in sympathy. "He was always quiet but since his mother left the family it's gotten worse."

"But why a knife? It doesn't make sense. He's not a violent kid," said Mr. Villa.

"Show off, maybe? Did you ask him?" asked Ms. Hopkins.

"He won't say anything. You know he was actually starting to make some progress. Rosa's been working with him, and he's started whispering the words beneath his breath when we're reading. Three letter words, but words."

"How's Rosa doing?" Mr. Brown interjected.

Mr. Villa, brightened, "Fantastic. I don't know how she does it. She's just zipping along. You know I have twelve holdovers from fourth grade last year. I've got one kid who crawls around on the floor. I've got two kids who don't know all the letters of the alphabet. The other day in my little "Hot Dogs" reading group."

"You call them, "Hot Dogs?" queried Brown.

"Yeah, each group has a name; "The Hot Dogs," "The Cool Cucumbers," and "The Rappers." The kids thought them up. So, I ask Willie to put together some word blends like S-T and E-W to make the word stew, B-R and E-W to make the word brew, and C-R and E-W to make the word crew. So he sounds them out, and I ask him if he knows what the word crew means. So, he says, "Oh yeah, like my brother he's in a crew."

"It's true," said Ms. Hopkins. "His brother is in the "Lords" gang."

Mr. Villa shook his head in dismay. "That's just great!" he said sarcastically. "I don't know. I just hope I can get through the year."

"Well, it'll be an accomplishment, Villa," said Ms. Hopkins. "Most people didn't think you'd last this long with that class."

"I'll make it. But I could use some phonics books," said Mr. Villa.

Ms. Hopkins grimaced. "They change the curriculum every two or three years, throw out the books, and get a new chancellor who wants to recreate the wheel. I'll see what I can do to rustle up some phonics books for you."

"Thanks, Hopkins," said Villa. "They tell me everything I teach is supposed to be geared toward the tests. Half my kids aren't ready for second-grade tests, let alone fourth grade."

"It's amazing anybody ever learns anything," said Brown as the bell rang indicating the end of the period.

Rosa and Luis sat together by the fence, watching the kids heading back to class.

"Luis, why did you bring the knife?" asked Rosa.

"Shantel, she keeps bothering me."

"Did you tell anyone?"

Luis shrugged his shoulders and shook his head no.

"Luis, you have to tell Mr. Villa. They're going to suspend you."

Luis shrugged again.

"She said she'd get me if I told. She took my money," said Luis.

"So you brought the knife?"

"I'm not afraid of her. She's just big."

"They're going to suspend you. Did they call your dad?" asked Rosa.

Luis nodded yes.

"C'mon," said Rosa. "We'd better go in. I think you should tell them what happened."

CHAPTER 28 – THE ENCOUNTER

Luis's father, Mr. Rodriguez, was a short, stocky man in his late forties. He had come to America from Guatemala as a teenager and apprenticed himself as a carpenter. He had worked hard, joined a union, and become a citizen. He had learned his craft well, but he still spoke only halting English. It had been difficult to get the morning off to come to school to see the principal, but Luis was his only son, and he was worried about him. Mr. Rodriguez was a proud man who wanted a son he could be proud of. What would he do if they suspended Luis? Who would take care of him? Mr. Villa, Luis's teacher, sat beside him. He liked Mr. Villa. He knew the teacher wanted the best for his son. He sat upright and rigid as the principal explained the situation.

"Mr. Villa, Mr. Rodriguez says the knife Luis brought to school was a fishing knife he gave to his son. He says Luis must have forgotten it in his backpack when they were fishing by the river on Sunday."

Mr. Villa wasn't buying it. "The kids say Luis brought it because Shantel threatened him."

"Mr. Villa, did he tell you that?" asked the principal.

"No, he won't say anything."

Mr. Cajas pushed the button on the intercom. "He's outside. I'll have him brought in. Ms. Stephenson, please send Luis in."

Luis tentatively opened the door. Mr. Cajas spoke in Spanish to Mr. Rodriguez and explained what Mr. Villa had said.

"Mr. Villa thinks one of the other children here has been threatening Luis and perhaps that is why he brought the knife. But Luis won't speak to us." Mr. Cajas pointed to a chair beside Luis's father. "Sit down here, Luis."

Luis slowly walked to the chair, sat down, and lowered his head so as not to meet his father's eyes.

Mr. Rodriguez looked at his son sternly and spoke to him in Spanish.

"Is it true what he says, Luis?"

Luis shrugged sheepishly. Mr. Rodriguez quickly leaned over to Luis and shook him violently.

"Is this how you behave to me? You shame me? Talk to me when I speak to you."
Luis was embarrassed. He began to breathe heavily as he looked up at his father.

"Yes," he said quietly.

"Yes, what?" demanded his father.

"She took my money."

Mr. Rodriguez was angry. "Mr. Cajas, is this the type of school you run? You allow the children to steal from each other?"

Mr. Cajas picked up the telephone and called for Shantel to be brought in. Ms. Hopkins knocked on the door and entered with Shantel by her side.

"Sit down, Shantel," said Mr. Cajas pointing to a chair. But Shantel did not sit. "Luis says you've been taking his money," said Mr. Cajas.

"He's a liar," shouted Shantel. "I never took nothing."

Mr. Rodriguez stood and faced Shantel. "My boy doesn't lie."

"You a freakin' liar, too," screamed Shantel.

Enraged, Mr. Rodriguez pointed his finger at Shantel.

"You touch my boy again, I'll take care of you," warned Mr. Rodriguez.

Shantel grabbed the chair in front of her and pushed it at Mr. Rodriguez's chair.

"You touch me, I'll sue you. I'll get you both. You liar. Liar!" yelled Shantel. She quickly turned on her heel and ran from the room.

Mr. Cajas jumped to his feet. "Shantel, get back here." By the time he reached the office door, Shantel was gone.

CHAPTER 29 – THE POLICE

It was a quiet afternoon; Luishana was washing the dishes, and Jorge was playing on the floor with his Legos. The knock at the door startled Luishana from her daydream. She wasn't expecting anyone. It would be hours before Rosa would be back from school. She looked through the peephole and saw a tall black man in his late forties and a small Hispanic woman, neither of whom she knew.

"Who is it?" asked Luishana.

"Police, ma'am. Open up please."

Luishana nervously looked around, straightened her dress, and opened the door, keeping the chain on.

"What is it?"

"I'm Detective Fredericks, and this is Ms. Jimenez," said the detective holding up his identification. "Are you Luishana Sanchez?"

"Yes."

"Mind if we come in?" asked the detective.

"Why? What for?" asked Luishana.

"You mind letting us in, ma'am, we need to talk to you? It's about Mrs. McMillan."

"Mrs. McMillan? One minute. All right."

Luishana removed the chain and opened the door.

"Is there anyone else here in the apartment?" asked Ms. Jimenez.

Luishana indicated Jorge at play. "No, just me and my son."

"Do you mind if we look?" asked the detective.

"It's just the two rooms, there's no one here. What do you want? What happened to Ms. McMillan?"

"You've been working for Mrs. McMillan?' asked the detective.

"Yes."

"Her apartment's been robbed."

"Robbed? When? I haven't been there since Monday. I go Monday and Friday. Today's my day off," said Luishana.

"So, you haven't seen her since Monday?" questioned Fredericks.

"Yes. I saw her Monday. I made lunch for her and did the laundry."

"How long have you been working for her?"

"Just a couple of months," replied Luishana.

"You're on welfare?" asked Ms. Jimenez.

A puzzled look crossed Luishana's face as a question came to mind. "Is that what this is about? She pays me a hundred dollars a week. That's all. I just didn't get to report it yet. I was going to."

"You'll have to come down to the station house, Ms. Sanchez," said the detective.

Luishana looked around nervously. "Wait, wait, wait! How long will this take? My daughter gets back from school at three-thirty."

"I'll meet her if that's necessary," said Ms. Jimenez. "I'm from Social Services."

CHAPTER 30 – THE PLAYGROUND

Rosa had decided to teach some of the self-defense techniques she had learned from Mee to Luis. Shantel had been suspended from school for a week, but she would be back. Luis and Rosa practiced together during lunchtime in the schoolyard. Latoya and Serena also wanted to learn. They put down their jump ropes and looked on as Rosa showed Luis how to sidestep a punch.

"Where'd you learn all this stuff? You take a martial arts class or somethin'?" asked Serena.

"No," said Rosa, "I look it up on the computer and practice."

"So that's how you did that stuff with that guy who tried to rip off our computers. That was so cool. You should have seen her, Luis. It was unbelievable," marveled Latoya. Rosa was enjoying her friends' admiration, although she also was feeling a little embarrassed about being in the spotlight. She just wanted to help Luis, not draw so much attention to herself. She was just about to demonstrate a wrist hold when Mr. Villa walked up to her.

"Rosa, the principal wants to see you. Come with me," said Mr. Villa.

"Don't tell me he can't open his e-mail again?" said Rosa.

Mr. Villa smiled. "No, I don't think that's it."

Going to the principal's office made Rosa nervous. When she and Mr. Villa entered, she immediately felt something was wrong. A strange woman was sitting in front of the principal's desk, and the principal looked very serious.

"Please, sit down, Rosa," said the principal.

Rosa sat. Mr. Villa stood beside her.

"I have some bad news for you, Rosa. Your mother's been arrested," said Mr. Cajas.

Rosa was stunned. "Arrested? Why? What happened?" she managed to blurt out.

The principal folded his hands in front of him. "I don't know any of the details. It seems the woman she's been working for was robbed recently and the police think your mother was involved."

"But she couldn't, Mami would never..." Rosa burst into tears.

Mr. Villa bent down beside Rosa and put his arm around her.

"Where is she?" asked Rosa.

Ms. Jimenez, the woman seated beside the principal, turned to Rosa and said, "She's at the police station."

"I want to see her. I want to see her," said Rosa.

"I'm afraid that won't be possible today," said Ms. Jimenez.

Mr. Cajas looked over at Rosa and then at Ms. Jimenez. "Rosa, this is Ms. Jimenez, she is from Social Services and is here to escort you home so you can get your things," explained Mr. Cajas.

"Where's Jorge? Where's my brother?" pleaded Rosa.

Ms. Jimenez stood up and faced Rosa. "He's being looked after by Social Services. Your mother asked that you be left in school here and has made arrangements to have you stay at your friend Latoya's home for the next seventy-two hours until things can be sorted out."

"What does that mean sorted out? I want to see my mother," sobbed Rosa.

CHAPTER 31 – SLEEPOVER

The brownstone Latoya lived in on West 124th St. was a single-family home. Her dad had bought it years ago and had it remodeled. On the top floor, he had made a workroom for himself that was part workshop and part office. It was filled with books, filing cabinets, and a desk piled high with papers. On one side of the room near the windows was a large table on which there were four model airplanes and drones of different sizes and colors. Latoya peeked inside the room to make sure her dad wasn't there. She led Rosa inside.

"You gotta see this. This is my dad's workshop," bragged Latoya.

She walked over to the planes and picked one up.

"Do they really fly?" asked Rosa.

"Yeah, they work great! My dad controls them with his laptop and a joystick."

Latoya's mom called from downstairs. "Girls, where are you? The cookies are ready."

"C'mon," said Latoya. "My mom makes great cookies."

Later that evening, Latoya and Rosa sat in their pajamas doing their homework on Latoya's bed. On Latoya's dresser was a model remote control airplane. She picked it up and pretended it was flying.

"Brrmmmmmm. Brrmmmm."

"Is that your dad's?" asked Rosa.

Latoya smiled proudly. "No, it's mine. My dad gave it to me. It's remote control; it really flies. We fly it sometimes in the park. I like to pretend like I can get in it and just fly out my window and all over the neighborhood. And I peek in at what everybody's doing; then I just fly away."

"Sounds like fun," said Rosa half-heartedly.

Latoya put down the plane.

"Maybe we could fly it this weekend if you want. I'm sure my dad will take us. I'm finished with my homework. Want to watch some television?"

"No," said Rosa, "I'm kind of tired."

"*Walking Dead*" entreated Latoya. "I watch it every week."

"Nuh-uh. No, thanks, I'll just stay here and play on my computer for a while."

"All right, Rosa, but come on down to the living room if you want to. My mom watches, too."

"I'd rather do stuff on the computer," said Rosa.

Latoya could hear the sadness in Rosa's voice. She went over to Rosa and spoke softly. "I'm sorry you're so sad, but I'm glad you're here. "

Rosa forced a smile. "Thanks."

Latoya turned and walked out of the room. Rosa put on her headphones and typed her code into the laptop.

"Mee, I need you. "

The computer lit up.

"Hello, Rosa."

"Did you find out where they're keeping my mom?"

"Yes, Rosa. She's in the women's detention center, downtown."

"What are we going to do, Mee?"

"That's the first time you've referred to us as *we*. It's a very interesting form of bonding. What shall "we" do?"

Rosa reeled off a list of all the things she was hoping for. "I'd like us to see my mom. I'd like us to get her out of jail. I'd like us to find my brother. I'd like us to go home."

"I understand," said Mee. "Perhaps tomorrow. She has a court-assigned lawyer who will represent her before the judge tomorrow. I have his e-mail address. I think we should send him an e-mail about your concerns."

"She didn't do it, did she? She didn't steal that lady's stuff, did she Mee?"

"I don't know, Rosa, but we'll try to find out. Did you get the package I sent you?"

Rosa took a small box from her backpack. She opened the box, and inside was a new mobile phone."

"How'd you get them to send me this?" asked Rosa.

"It was a free offer. I just filled in the electronic blanks. It's activated."

"Isn't that stealing?"

Mee sounded surprised. "Stealing? I don't think so. It was a free trial offer. I get free offers all the time, and junk mail too. I want to look after you, Rosa, and that means you must be able to stay in touch with me at all times."

Rosa pondered this for a moment, then powered up the cell phone.

"Thank you, Mee."

"You're welcome, Rosa. It has a built-in camera."

"Cool!"

CHAPTER 32 – THE DEAL

Carlos stacked the paintings he had stolen from Ms. McMillan's apartment against the wall of the one-room efficiency he rented in Spanish Harlem. He opened Mrs. McMillan's rosewood jewelry box, emptied the contents onto the cheap, beat-up card table that served as his kitchen table, and examined each piece. Smiling to himself, he tried to estimate their worth. The question was how could he get rid of them without being caught. He quickly thought of Miguel, rang him up, and told him about the haul.

"Miguel, it's not just jewelry. I've got paintings, real paintings, that I think could be worth a lot."

"What am I gonna do with paintings?" asked Miguel.

"They're original. They're worth a lot of money."

"To whom?" sneered Miguel.

Carlos was taken aback. "I don't know, that's why I called you."

"What am I, Sotheby's?" laughed Miguel.

"No, I mean, yeah! You got good taste, Miguel. Gimme a break, take a look, see what you think."

"All right, Carlos. I'll let you know when."

Miguel hung up the phone. Carlos fell back on the couch and went to sleep.

CHAPTER 33 – BACK HOME

Three days after the robbery, Ms. Jimenez brought Rosa back to Rosa's apartment. Rosa put her book bag on her bed, got out some fresh clothing, and changed into it. Together they went to the kitchen and waited.

"I thought you said my mom would be here?"

"She'll be here any minute, Rosa. She went to get your brother first."

"Is he okay?"

"He's fine, Rosa," said Ms. Jimenez.

The moment the key turned in the lock, Rosa jumped up and ran to the door.

"Mami! Mami!"

The door swung open, and there stood Luishana holding Jorge in her arms. Luishana put Jorge down and embraced Rosa.

"Baby, oh I'm so glad to see you," beamed Luishana. "Are you okay?"

Rosa burst into tears.

"Yes. I was so worried."

Rosa grabbed Jorge and hugged him. Ms. Jimenez came from the kitchen and stood beside them in the dark hallway.

"She's been very good, Ms. Sanchez. She's kept up with her schoolwork."

"Thank you, for looking after her, Ms. Jimenez."

"Here's my card. If you have any problems or if you change your mind, call me," said Ms. Jimenez. "Goodbye, Rosa."

"Goodbye," said Rosa.

Ms. Jimenez smiled at Rosa and walked past her and out the door. Luishana shut the door after her and turned on the hallway light. As she turned back to Rosa, Rosa jumped up into her arms. Luishana hugged her and smiled.

"What did she mean, change your mind?" asked Rosa.

Luishana put Rosa down, and together they walked into the living room and sat down on the couch. "She wants me to put you in a foster home in case I'm convicted and sent to jail," explained Luishana. "But I won't, I won't, I won't. I didn't do it, and I won't lose you. You're all I've got." Luishana pulled Jorge and Rosa to her and hugged them.

"You won't leave us?" pleaded Rosa.

"Never, baby," smiled Luishana as tears welled up in her eyes.

CHAPTER 34 – THE CASE

Mr. Mendoza was Luishana's court-appointed attorney. Like so many attorneys who make their living by representing the poor, he had many cases that paid little and had little time to prepare for each. His small basement office was stacked with folders and papers. Luishana sat before the tired, heavyset man as he rummaged through his files.

"It's here somewhere. Oh yes, here it is, Luishana Sanchez."

He thumbed through the file.

"I didn't do it," offered Luishana.

"Of course not, but let's see. They found a silk shirt belonging to Ms. McMillan among your things."

"But I explained that. I was supposed to bring it to the cleaners, and I forgot."

"Ms. McMillan doesn't remember telling you that, Luishana."

"She doesn't remember anything. She told me if I see things lying around that need cleaning to bring them in. I was just doing my job."

"And then there's the non-reporting of the job. You're supposed to go on workfare."

"Mr. Mendoza, can they lock me up for that?"

"No, the judge won't want to separate you from your family. But they won't drop the burglary charge. The paintings and jewelry were insured for more than a million dollars."

Luishana was incredulous, "Really?"

"Really. The insurance company's not going to pay out the money without an investigation. If you know anything about it? If we could recover the goods, then maybe...".

"But I don't know anything about it. I didn't have anything to do with it," pleaded Luishana.

"Then who could? Somebody got in there with a key. There was no forced entry. Somebody knew about those paintings."

"I don't know, I don't know, I don't know," wept Luishana.

CHAPTER 35 – MEE'S DISGUISE

Rosa's new cell phone was a great convenience. She no longer had to carry around her laptop to talk with Mee. She could just ring him up like any other friend. At recess, she found a secluded spot and called.

"Mee?"

"Yes, Rosa."

"They keep going after my mom. It's making her crazy. Did you find out anything?"

"I looked into the history of the paintings that were taken. Hudson River School paintings. Quite valuable."

"But where are they?"

"Carlos Pinero has them," said Mee.

"Carlos, who my mother knows?" asked Rosa.

"Yes, he's made an appointment to sell them to your uncle."

Rosa was surprised. "My uncle Miguel? What's he got to do with it?"

"Carlos often does work for him," said Mee.

"How did you find all that out?"

"I listened to his phone. I saw him here with your mother one day and put him on my suspect list and listened in on his phone."

Rosa couldn't believe what she was hearing. "You tapped his phone? Mee, don't you need a court order for that?"

"I'm not the police, Rosa," said Mee.

Rosa thought about that for a minute. She wondered what it meant if you could listen to anybody's phone anytime you wanted. But then she came back to her own problems and asked Mee, "So what do we do?"

"Well, we could try to recover the stolen goods, but that might get you into trouble, or we could have him arrested, or you could introduce him to Mee."

"But I thought you wouldn't talk to anybody but me?"

"I'll wear a disguise," said Mee with almost childish enthusiasm.

"But Mee, you don't have a body."

Mee's voice grew deeper.

"But I do have a voice."

"Oh!" said Rosa. "Can you sound like anyone you want to?"

"Yes," said Mee. "I'm very good at imitating sounds."

CHAPTER 36 - UNCLE MIGUEL

As soon as school let out, Rosa went to visit her uncle Miguel. Her uncle was surprised and happy to see Rosa. He hugged Rosa and invited her into his spacious, nicely furnished apartment. Rosa settled on the sofa, and Miguel sat on a chair facing her.

"It's nice to see you, Rosa. I haven't seen you in a long time. Would you like some milk and cookies? I think there's some cake."

"No thanks, Uncle Miguel. "I need to talk to you about my mom."

"She's not my favorite subject, Rosa. I tried to take care of you, but she wouldn't take my help."

"I know, Uncle Miguel. She doesn't want to be involved in your business. She's doing it for us. Jorge and me."

"I understand, but I only want to help," said Miguel.

"Will you help me?" asked Rosa.

"How, Rosa?"

"I have a friend I want you to talk to. His name is Mr. Mee."

Rosa took out her cell phone and punched in her code. She placed the phone on speaker and handed it to her uncle.

"All right."

"Hello," Mr. Sanchez," said Mee in a deep masculine voice. "We have a proposition for you. We know Mr. Carlos Pinero has certain property which he is planning to sell you."

Miguel was startled.

"Hey, who is this? Is this the police? If this is a sting you gotta' tell me."

"Rest assured, Mr. Sanchez, this is to your benefit, otherwise, I would not have allowed Rosa to come."

"Mr. Mee sounds like a Chinese name. You Chinese? You don't sound Chinese."

"And you don't sound Hispanic."

. Would you prefer I speak with an accent?"

Miguel laughed.

"No! What's the deal, Mr. Mee?"

"We need the paintings and jewelry returned and a confession from Carlos Pinero."

"You expect me to turn in Carlos?"

"He betrayed us, Uncle Miguel," interjected Rosa.

"I didn't know about this, Rosa. But I can't go to the police."

"Then what? We have to clear Mom, or they'll put me and Jorge in a home," pleaded Rosa.

"I don't know, Rosa," said Miguel.

"It's simple really," said Mee. "I have a plan where you can return the paintings to the insurance company and collect the reward, providing you share it with Rosa and her family. Or we can just have the police pick up Carlos."

"Tell me more," said Miguel. "Let's see if we can work it out with the insurance company. Okay, Rosa?"

Rosa smiled and nodded her head in approval.

CHAPTER 37 – COMPUTER TROUBLE

On Monday morning, when Rosa got off the school bus, she could feel something was wrong. The kids standing in line were even noisier than usual. As soon as she made her way to her line, Serena ran over to her.

"Rosa, did you hear the computers are missing? They're all gone. All the laptops in the computer lab. C'mon."

Serena grabbed Rosa by the arm, and the girls slipped away from their line, worked their way into the building, and ran down the hallway to the computer lab. Mr. Brown was standing by the doorway talking to Mr. Diaz, a plainclothes detective. The girls peeked in and listened. Mr. Brown pointed to the window.

"I came in this morning and the computers were all gone. They must've gotten in through the window. The doors were all locked. I'm sure I locked those windows before I left."

Detective Diaz walked over to the windows and looked out. "They probably lowered themselves down from the roof with a rope. Was anyone in here after you left?"

"Sometimes some of the teachers stay late, and the maintenance guys come in, but they don't usually open the windows," offered Brown.

Rosa and Serena walked into the computer lab and approached Mr. Brown.

"Did they take them all?" asked Rosa.

"Yes, all the laptops. You girls better get to your rooms. You'll be late," said Mr. Brown.

Serena and Rosa looked at each other and ran off down the hall together as the bell rang.

Rosa couldn't wait to tell Mee about what had happened at school. Of course, Mee probably already knew. There wasn't much that went on at Rosa's school that Mee wasn't aware of. As soon as Mr. Villa finished roll call, Rosa got a pass to go to the girls' room and phoned Mee.

"They took all the computers, Mee. You've got to help us find them."

"Yes," said Mee. "I can do that."

"Do you know who took them?" asked Rosa.

"Not yet. But all they have to do is go on the Internet with one of them and I'll know where it's located."

"Cool," said Rosa. "See you after school."

CHAPTER 38 – MORE TROUBLE

It was a cool evening. Luis was on his way to the bodega for the groceries his father had asked him to buy for their dinner. He looked across the street at the construction site where a couple of old half-demolished brownstones had been fenced off. The sign on the buildings said they were being remodeled, but work had stopped on them weeks ago for some reason. Luis had just passed the site when he looked back and spotted Shantel as she ducked into a hole in the fence and entered one of the buildings. *What is she doing in there?* he thought to himself. Luis crossed the street and peered through the hole in the fence. He didn't really know why but he crawled inside and hid in the shadows. From his vantage point, he saw Shantel walk to the staircase and call out.

"Julio, where are you?"

Julio called down from the second floor. "That you Shantel? We're up here."

Shantel ran up the battered staircase and walked into a half-demolished room at the head of the stairs. There stood Julio and Carlos. Julio, flashlight in hand, threw back a dust-covered painting tarpaulin to reveal dozens of laptop computers.

"These are the goods, Carlos," said Julio.

"Who's she?' asked Carlos, indicating Shantel.

"It's okay, this is my cuz' I was tellin' you about. Shantel this is my connection, Carlos. Carlos, he's gonna sell the computers for us."

Shantel nodded, "Hi."

Carlos nodded his head in acknowledgment at Shantel. Julio replaced the tarpaulin over the computers and then covered them with bits of broken plaster and sticks.

"Julio, be careful with my merchandise," warned Carlos. "I'll be back tomorrow night to pick them up."

"Don't worry, Carlos; I'll take good care of them!" said Julio.

"Let's go!" said Carlos.

From the shadows, in the stillness of the building, Luis could hear everything they said. He stepped into a shadowy corner behind the staircase as Carlos, Shantel, and Julio came down the stairs.

"Be careful coming and goin' from here. Make sure nobody spots you," Carlos reminded them.

"Yeah, sure," said Julio. "We'll be careful."

Carlos turned off his flashlight. "Put out your flashlights."

Luis watched as they crawled back out through the fence. He moved out slowly from his hiding place and made his way upstairs in the darkness. It only took a few minutes of searching before he spotted the tarpaulin. He pulled it back and picked up one of the computers. But when he turned to leave, he found three flashlights shining in his face. Carlos was the first to speak.

"Hey kid, there's no free samples."

Shantel pinned Luis's arms as Carlos grabbed the computer from him.

"Hey, let go!" cried Luis.

"This is the kid got me suspended," sneered Shantel.

Julio looked at Carlos, "What are we gonna do with him?"

Carlos grabbed some old rope sitting by the tarpaulin. "Tie him up."

Shantel grabbed the rope and tied him up while Julio stood by watching.

"You bad, Shantel, you know that?" smiled Julio.

Carlos wasn't smiling. "We'll have to get rid of him."

"You don't mean kill him?" stammered Julio.

"You'd rather let him blab?" said Carlos.

Shantel turned a sickly face toward Julio. She hadn't counted on this.

CHAPTER 39 - INSURANCE

Carlos wasn't sure what to ask for the paintings he had brought to Miguel's apartment. He didn't really like the paintings particularly, but they seemed to have nice frames. Still, he knew that whatever they were worth, Miguel would try to get them for nothing if he could. The best thing would be to make Miguel think he really liked them.

"They are beautiful, aren't they, Miguel?"

Miguel was surprised at how fine the paintings actually were. Still, he had a part to play.

"Not exactly my taste, Carlos." They sell this stuff on the street for practically nothing."

"But the pearls and stones, the jewelry, are good."

"Listen, Carlos, I'll give you $5,000 for the lot," proffered Miguel.

"The jewels are worth at least fifty grand. Gimme, twenty-five thousand and I'll throw in the paintings."

Miguel wasn't negotiating. "Don't act crazy. I'll give you five thousand, which is more than you deserve. You took this from the place my sister-in-law's working; you're lucky I don't just put a bullet in your sick brain."

Carlos could see he had no leverage. "All right, it's a deal, but only because it's you."

"How'd you break in? It's a doorman building, isn't it?" asked Miguel as he counted out the money into Carlos's hand.

"I copied her key. She didn't know anything. I went in the back. The super leaves the door to the basement open for a few hours after he takes out the garbage. The old lady was off at some appointment; it was a piece of cake." Carlos took the money.

"You are never to come near my sister-in-law again. You understand me, Carlos?" warned Miguel.

"I didn't think they'd bother her. I didn't mean nothin'." Carlos turned back to the couch where he had left his backpack. "Look what else I got, Miguel."

Carlos opened up the backpack and took out one of the stolen laptops.

A look of curiosity crossed Miguel's face. "Nice. How many you got?"

"Thirty-two. All perfect. Brand new."

Miguel's expression changed from curiosity to anger. "Thirty-two? That's just what was stolen from my niece's school. You're screwing with my family again."

Miguel took out a gun and pointed it at Carlos's head.

"Whoa! Be cool, Miguel! I didn't do it. I'm just the middleman."

"You bring them all here by tomorrow night or you get nothin'. Half my people's kids go to that school, there will be no end of trouble if I show up with their kids' computers. What're you, crazy? Give me back that five grand, so I make sure you show up here with those computers."

Carlos reluctantly reached into his pocket and started to hand the money back to Miguel.

"I need at least a thousand just to get them," pleaded Carlos. I got expenses.

Miguel took the cash, counted out a thousand dollars, and handed it to Carlos.

"Here's a thousand, now get outta here."

Carlos started to pack up the computer.

"Leave the computer," said Miguel.

Carlos looked at the computer and then at the gun in Miguel's hand.

"Miguel, you and me are okay, aren't we? I didn't mean to involve your family. You know I didn't."

"I know," said Miguel in a cold voice. "Now go. I'll see you when you bring the computers. Now go."

Carlos walked slowly to the door and left. The door had no sooner closed behind Carlos when Mr. Stephenson, the insurance adjuster, came out of the bedroom. Miguel turned towards him with a questioning look. "So, you heard enough to get your insurance company off my sisters-in-law Luishana's back?"

Mr. Stephenson walked over to the paintings and began to inspect them. "Yes. We could have the police pick up Carlos and the computers if you'd like."

"That's not necessary. But it'd be nice if you returned them for us. I don't want to be involved," said Miguel.

"I can do that," answered the adjustor.

CHAPTER 40 - MISSING

The school day was over. Kids streamed out the front door of P.S. 101 and into the street. Rosa waited for Latoya to buy a churro from the cart outside school.

"Want a bite?" asked Latoya.

Rosa nodded yes and took a bite of the sweet pasty flour dough. Serena came up beside her.

"Rosa, did you hear about Luis?"

"No, he wasn't in class."

"I just saw his dad in the office talking to a guard. He's missing."

"Luis is missing?"

"I heard his dad say he didn't come home last night."

"Are you sure?" asked Rosa.

"That's what I heard," confirmed Serena.

The kids started to walk down the block toward Latoya's house when Shantel came running at them with her arm extended like a football player trying to smash his way through the line. The kids barely stepped aside in time to avoid her. She continued running down the block.

"I thought she was suspended," said Latoya.

" She is," said Serena. "She hasn't been in school this week."

"Forget her," said Latoya. "You guys want to come over my house for a while?"

"Sure," said Rosa.

The kids continued walking down Amsterdam Avenue toward Latoya's house. Near 126th street, they spotted Shantel.

"Oh, no! There she is again," grimaced Latoya.

"Maybe we should cross the street," said Serena.

"No, just ignore her. Maybe she won't bother us," said Latoya.

Shantel stood on the corner, shaking her head as she watched the girls pass. She looked as though she were trying to make up her mind about something. Finally, she called out.

"Rosa, come here. I got something to tell you."

Latoya whispered to Rosa, "Don't listen! Keep walking."

"Come on, I'm not going to hurt you. It's important, Rosa."

Rosa hesitated. The other girls tried to pull Rosa along, but she stood fast, looking at Shantel.

"Don't be so afraid, I'm not going to bite you," beckoned Shantel.

Rosa pulled away from the girls.

"What do you want?" asked Rosa.

"Just come here for a second. I just want to whisper something to you," said Shantel.

Rosa walked up to her. Shantel whispered to Rosa.

"It's about Luis."

Latoya called to Rosa. "Come on, Rosa."

"In a minute," Rosa called back.

"You should come with us, Rosa," said Serena.

"You go ahead, I'll catch up," shouted Rosa.

"The girls shrugged and walked on, anxious to be away from Shantel. Shantel looked at Rosa not quite sure of what she was about to do.

"I know where Luis is," confided Shantel in a low voice. "But I'll only show you."

Rosa looked dubious but quickly made her decision. She called after the girls as they hesitatingly walked away.

"I'll see you later."

Shantel seemed worried about what she wanted to say. "I'll show you where Luis is but only if you promise not to tell and make him promise not to tell."

"Tell what?" asked Rosa.

"What happened!" blurted out Shantel.

"What did happen, Shantel?"

"Only if you swear. Otherwise, they'll kill him and me, too."

"All right, Shantel, I swear," promised Rosa.

"C'mon, follow me."

Shantel turned and ran down the block, signaling Rosa to follow. Rosa ran after her.

CHAPTER 41 – READY OR NOT

Shantel led Rosa to the break in the fence of the construction site where Luis was being held and motioned to Rosa to follow her. Rosa hesitated and looked at her questioningly.

"Well, do you want to find him or not?" asked Shantel.

Shantel bent down and squeezed through the hole in the fence. She grabbed Rosa by the wrist and pulled her through.

"Come on!"

Once inside the building, Rosa looked cautiously about her. Walls to some of the rooms had been knocked down, doors hung off their hinges, and lighting fixtures were torn from their sockets. Part of the ceiling was broken through, so you could see through the ceiling to the floor above. Shafts of sunlight streamed into the building through the holes in the roof, walls, and back windows. Dust, dirt, and construction materials were everywhere.

"Where is he? Luis, are you here? Luis?" Rosa shouted.

Shantel stood at the foot of the staircase. "He's upstairs. Come on. I'll show you."

Shantel led Rosa up the dilapidated staircase to the second floor.

"Come on! Come on!" urged Shantel. "He's on the third floor, the last room on the right."

The kids ran up the stairs to the third floor, where Shantel came to an abrupt halt and pointed down the hallway. "He's down there in the last room. Go on!"

Rosa warily made her way down the hallway, slowly pushed the door open, and entered. Luis sat tied and gagged on the floor. Shantel called after Rosa from the doorway.

"Remember you have to make him promise not to tell."

Rosa ran to Luis and removed his gag.

Shantel walked up to Luis and towered over him. "Rosa's going to let you go, but only if you swear not to tell on me or Julio. You tell I let you go; I'll get you for sure. You understand?" threatened Shantel.

Fear, hate, panic, and confusion played across Luis's face. He began to tremble with rage.

Rosa tried to comfort him, "It's all right, Luis. It's all right."

Shantel walked back to the doorway.

"You better make him swear."

"I will," said Rosa.

"You better," said Shantel, turning on her heel and running down the hall. Rosa pulled at the ropes holding Luis. The knots were tight, and it wasn't easy. Finally, they gave way. Luis's wrists were red and sore.

"Are you all right?" asked Rosa.

Luis nodded his head and shakily got to his feet. Rosa led Luis down the hallway.

"What happened, Luis? How did you get here?" asked Rosa. Luis remained silent. Luis and Rosa walked down the stairs. When they got to the second floor, Luis grabbed Rosa by the arm and pulled her into the half-demolished room where the computers were hidden.

"Come! Come," pleaded Luis as Rosa held back.

Luis drew back the tarpaulin and uncovered the laptops. Rosa walked over beside Luis.

"The school's computers. Did Shantel steal them?" asked Rosa.

Luis nodded.

"Shantel and her cousin Julio," said Luis.

Rosa looked at the computers and then at Luis. "We better get going. I swore I wouldn't tell on her. You have got to swear too."

Luis's lips tightened, and his face became red with anger, as he shook his head no.

"You've got to; for me. We can't tell. She said they'd kill you if you told, Luis."

"I don't care. I'm not afraid," stammered Luis.

"I know, Luis. But you got to promise, for me. I don't want anything to happen to you. And now they'd go after me too. She helped us. I wouldn't know you were here otherwise. Swear! Swear!"

Luis didn't want to swear, but he knew in his heart that he owed so much to Rosa. He couldn't let her be hurt. Reluctantly, he gave in. "All right, for you, I swear," he said.

Rosa gave out a sigh of relief. "C'mon let's get out of here, Luis."

Luis followed Rosa to the top of the stairs and looked down. There in front of them stood Julio and Carlos.

Julio looked at Rosa, a mean smile on his face. "Well, look who's here."

"It's Mannie's kid. What're you doin' here?" demanded Carlos.

Rosa looked around her for a way out. "We sometimes play here; I was just foolin' around."

"Well, that's too bad for you, ain't it?" muttered Julio.

Rosa and Luis quickly backed up onto the landing. Julio and Carlos swiftly followed. Julio made a grab for Rosa, but Rosa was too quick. She ducked beneath his open arms and picked up a broken piece of scrap wood on the floor.

"Run, Luis, run," shouted Rosa, but Luis just stood frozen in place.

Rosa stood her ground, facing off with Julio. Julio made a feint toward Rosa and pulled back.

"So, you like to play with sticks?" mocked Julio.

Julio picked up a metal bar from the floor and swung it at Rosa. Rosa jumped out of the way and ran around a broken table that had been left in the room. She pushed over the table and ducked behind it, shielding herself from the metal bar Julio swung at her again and again. She jumped to her feet and deflected the metal bar with her stick once, twice, until it was knocked from her hand. She ducked again as the metal bar sailed over her head and left a sizable dent in the plaster wall. She knocked over a wooden chair as she tried to escape from Julio. Carlos ran up behind Rosa and tried to grab her, but Rosa sidestepped, and Carlos fell to the floor. Julio's metal bar crashed to the ground, barely missing Rosa. Seeing Rosa was in danger, Luis jumped on Julio's back but was quickly tossed aside.

"Go, Rosa, run!" screamed Luis.

Julio lunged at Rosa again and again, backing her into the partially demolished kitchen area. She grabbed a broken metal kitchen cabinet door lying on the ground and used it as a shield to ward off Julio's blows.

Seeing an opportunity, she hurled the cabinet door against Julio's legs. He toppled over flat on his back, dropping the pole. Rosa picked up the metal bar and faced Julio as he slowly got to his feet. The two stood glaring at each other for a moment, each planning their next move, when Carlos reappeared in the doorway, pointing a gun at Rosa's head.

"Put down the pole or I'll put a bullet in your head. Now!"

Rosa dropped the pole.

"Lie down on your stomach. You too, Luis," commanded Carlos.

"Julio, tie her up."

Julio quickly found some rope and tied Luis and Rosa's hands behind their backs, then pulled them toward the radiator and tied them to it.

"Carlos, what are we going to do with them?" asked Julio.

"Well, we can't just leave them, someone might find 'em, and we can't let 'em go. Miguel will kill me if he finds out."

"You better let us go! You'll be in a lot of trouble if my uncle finds out," shouted Rosa.

"Shut up you little brat! I'm gonna take good care of you," snarled Julio.

"Julio, take some of that sacking and gag her." Julio ripped some of the sacking from a bag of carpenter's nails and tied it around Rosa and Luis's mouths.

"We're going to have to burn this place down, make it look like an accident. You like fires, Julio?"

Something crazy began to dance in Julio's eyes, "I love fires," he said.

"No one can blame us for an accident," said Carlos.

Carlos looked about the room and noticed the backpack Rosa had dropped during the fight. He picked it up and rummaged through it. At the bottom of the bag, he found her cell phone. He walked over to Rosa and pulled down her gag.

"Cool phone. What's the password?"

Rosa was defiant. "I'm not telling you."

Carlos was in no mood for an argument. "Oh, you'll tell me, or I'll kill you both now."

Rosa relented. "Mee."

"Yes, you, both of you."

"No, the password's M-E-E followed by my name R-O-S-A."

Carlos tapped in the letters.

"Yeah, that works. Thanks, I needed a new phone," quipped Carlos. "Julio come with me, we need to pack up the computers and get them downstairs."

CHAPTER 42 - NIGHT

The sun had set, and night was coming on. Rosa and Luis had been moved to the top floor of the old building and left there while Carlos and Julio shifted their stolen goods downstairs. Bound hand and foot and lashed to a steam pipe, somehow Rosa managed to squirm about till she faced Luis. She rubbed her nose against his gag until it came loose. Luis, in turn, pulled with his teeth at the sacking around Rosa's mouth till it loosened. In a very soft voice, Rosa whispered to Luis, "I'm going to try to bite through the rope around your hands. They might come back soon. We have to hurry. Hold still."

Rosa's mother was worried. Rosa had never stayed out late without letting her know where she was. She called her friends' homes and finally called the police.

"No, she didn't come home. I have no idea where she is. She was supposed to go to a friend's house after school but she's not there. They left her on 126th street about three-thirty. No one's seen her since."

Carlos thought he was in luck when he found a parking space for his old van just a dozen yards from the construction site. The moonlight and street lamplight flooded through the chinks in the walls of the old building. Carlos made his way inside the fence, where he found Julio playing with a pink ball. Julio doused the pink ball with a bottle of lighter fluid and set it ablaze. The ball flared up into a bright blue flame.

"Beautiful, isn't it? I love fires," smiled Julio.

Julio kicked the burning ball around with his foot.

Carlos turned on his flashlight and let its light play over the broken wooden floor tiles till he found what he was looking for. He walked over to a pile of old rags and paint cans that had been stored in a corner beside a half-broken wall.

"Julio, stop playing around. Put that out. We've got to make this look like an accident, spontaneous combustion. We pile these rags together then toss on a little lighter fluid and poof. They'll think it was the fumes and stuff that started the fire."

Julio picked up the extinguished ball and tossed it in the air. Carlos pulled out the cell phone he had taken from Rosa's backpack. He flicked it open and tapped in Miguel's number.

"Hi, Miguel. I'll be there in an hour." Carlos turned back to Julio. "C'mon my van's outside. Help me load the computers in. Where's your cousin, Shantel? She was supposed to be helping."

"Her grandma's been watching her like a hawk since she didn't come home the night we took the computers. She hid out in the coat closet in the computer room, then opened the windows for me."

"Yeah, that was clever," chuckled Carlos.

The ropes were thick and tasted awful, but Rosa ground her teeth into them again and again till they softened, and she could spit out a strand or two. Piece by piece, she worked methodically till her jaws ached, but finally, one of the ropes gave way, and Luis was free. Luis pulled at the knots that bound Rosa. Every creak in the old building was a reminder that their captors were nearby and might burst in on them at any moment.

"Hurry, they may come back," whispered Rosa. They could hear the muffled voices of Carlos and Julio as they walked up and down the stairs carrying the computers to Carlos's van.

"We gotta make it look like they fell or something. Like they were playing in here and maybe like where the ceiling's broke through, the floor gave way and they fell," mused Carlos.

"Then we torch the place?" asked Julio.

Luis finally managed to pull apart the knots tying Rosa's hands, and she soon freed her feet. Rosa and Luis quietly walked to the door, opened it a crack, and peeked through. They stealthily made their way to the staircase. They could hear the voices of Carlos and Julio returning. Rosa put her hand to her lips and motioned for Luis to follow her into another room at the other end of the hallway.

The kids pressed themselves flat against the wall as Julio and Carlos passed by them. Carlos panned his flashlight along the walls. Julio walked in front of Carlos and opened the door to the room where the kids had been held captive.

"Carlos, they're gone," cried an alarmed Julio.

Carlos pushed past Julio into the room. "What? Where could they go? They have to be here."

Carlos reached into his jacket and pulled out his gun.

"If they didn't come down the stairs, they've got to be hiding here somewhere."

Julio turned and walked down the hallway. He kicked open the door to the next room and played the flashlight over the walls. Nothing stirred.

"Julio, go downstairs! Make sure they don't get out; I'll search room to room."

"Okay."

"Hurry," said Carlos.

Julio turned and ran down the stairs.

"Come on out. We were only playing. We're gonna let you go. Come on before someone gets hurt," entreated Carlos.

Rosa signaled to Luis to be quiet and pointed to a half-open window at the back of the room that led to the fire escape. The kids tiptoed towards the window. The window was jammed, but Rosa managed to crawl through the partial opening and outside onto the fire escape. She motioned for Luis to follow her. He was barely through when Carlos burst into the room.

Carlos, catching a glimpse of Luis through the window, called after him. "Yo, Luis. Hold up, buddy."

Carlos ran to the window and peered through as Luis and Rosa fled up the steps. Carlos snapped open his cell phone and called Julio.

"Julio, they're trapped; they're going for the roof. Take the stairs and meet me."

Carlos managed to push the window up high enough to climb out onto the fire escape in pursuit.

It had been an unusually quiet night at the police station when the desk clerk answered a call for help.

"You say you heard screams from a building on 126th street. 61 West 126th street. A partially demolished building? Could you give me your name please? M-E-E. Mr. Mee can I get a number from you? You don't have a number, then how are you calling? A pay phone, gotcha. Can I have the pay phone's number then? Thanks. We'll send someone to check it right away."

Rosa and Julio bounded up the fire escape to the roof. They raced around the roof, looking for a way out.

Officer Jackson and Officer Gwynnis were cruising down 125th street when they got the call on their police radio. "Reported disturbance at 61 West 126th Street. Proceed to the location."

Latoya and her family were watching television and weren't aware that the propeller on her toy airplane had begun to turn. In Latoya's father's study, the propellers on the other half-dozen planes and drones also started to spin. One by one, the planes and drones lifted off the tabletop and made their way out of the window.

Rosa and Luis raced around the rooftop, looking for an escape. They noticed the roof door to the staircase and ran towards it, but a moment before they reached it, the door burst open, and Julio stood in front of them. Carlos appeared behind them on the fire escape. They were trapped. Suddenly they heard a buzzing above their heads, and a drone descended at high speed from the sky and dive-bombed toward Julio. Julio ducked in the nick of time to escape the drone and was about to get up when Luis dove at Julio's legs, knocking him over. Julio, stunned by the move, was momentarily disoriented.

Rosa pulled Luis to his feet and dragged him to the stairs. Carlos and Julio were right behind them. When they reached the third landing, Julio jumped the flight of stairs and landed on Rosa and Luis, knocking them to the ground.

Julio, Rosa, and Luis grappled with each other. They rolled over and over on the floor, dangerously close to the hole in the ceiling that dropped three stories to the ground floor below. Carlos stood over them laughing, then fired his gun in the air.

"Enough! Get up!" shouted Carlos and fired again.

Officer Jackson pulled the squad car to the curb when the first shot went off. The two policemen jumped from their vehicle, guns drawn. Jackson called for backup. Gwynnis grabbed a bullhorn from the backseat.

"This is the police. Whoever's in there come out now with your hands in the air," commanded Gwynnis.

Carlos pulled Luis to his feet and threw him toward Julio.

"It's the police, Carlos. What're we gonna do?" stammered Julio.

Carlos turned on Rosa, "This is your fault, you little brat."

Gun in hand, Carlos tried to grab Rosa, but suddenly the drones and airplanes were all over the room. The propeller from the first airplane bit into Carlos's hand. He yelled in pain.

"What the hell!" screamed Carlos as his gun dropped to the floor. A drone flew towards Carlos's head, barely missing him. The drone circled back for a second dive. Carlos covered his head with his hands and scurried for the stairs as two planes dive-bombed towards him. Julio tried to swat the planes down but slipped and fell towards the hole in the floor. Julio desperately grabbed at pieces of wood and broken plaster as he tried to stop himself from falling through the hole. At the last moment, he managed to grab an exposed piece of pipe and dangled in mid-air, a three-story fall below him. Luis stood over him.

"Now, I'm going to get you. Now, it's your turn."

Luis put his foot on Julio's hand and began to press down, but Rosa pulled him back.

"Stop it; you'll kill him, Luis."

Rosa dragged Luis back from the edge.

"He was going to kill us," shouted Luis.

"You can't kill him," screamed Rosa.

The planes and drones circled overhead then descended toward Julio for the kill. Rosa stepped in the path of the planes, and they veered off.

"No, you mustn't. He's helpless," cried Rosa.

The drones hovered for a moment, then flew up the stairs, where they continued to hover. The planes circled the room. Rosa bent down to grab Julio's wrist. She pulled with all her might, but Julio was too heavy for her to lift.

"You've got to help me, Luis. I can't do this alone."

Luis stood back, shaking his head in defiance. Julio hung from the pipe as it started to break. He begged for help.

"Help me up, help."

"Luis, you've got to help," called Rosa.

"He was going to kill us, Rosa," objected Luis.

Rosa was desperate. She could see the pipe holding Julio slowly wrenching free. She looked down at the three-story fall below.

"But not now, not now, he can't. Help me! I can't do this by myself, Luis."

Rosa started to slip forward. Julio, beginning to lose his grip on the pipe, started to pull Rosa towards the hole. Rosa held on with both hands, refusing to let him go. Luis hesitated a moment longer, but then realizing Rosa might be pulled to her death, reached down and grabbed Julio's other arm, and together they dragged him from the hole. Exhausted, Julio lay on his back, staring up at Rosa and Luis. An almost inaudible sound crossed his lips.

"Thanks," he said.

Carlos ran down the last flight of stairs, two at a time, as a drone buzzed around his head. Another drone attacked him from the foot of the stairs hitting his leg. Carlos went tumbling down the staircase and crashed to the ground as officers Jackson and Gwynnis entered the building.

Carlos let out a loud groan as he tried to rise but couldn't; his leg was broken in several places.

"Don't try to move," cautioned Jackson.

Gwynnis, hearing the commotion above, raised his flashlight and let it shine through the broken ceiling. Luis and Rosa peered down at him.

"You kids all right?" asked the officer.

The planes and drones circled up the stairs and out through the broken windows of the dilapidated building. Jackson caught a shadowy glimpse of the last drone as it made its way out the door behind him and into the night sky.

"What the hell was that?" wondered Jackson.

Gwynnis shone his flashlight on the empty doorway.

"Probably bats," answered Gwynnis.

CHAPTER 43 – BACK HOME

The police arrested Julio and Carlos and drove Luis and Rosa home. Rosa was exhausted but so excited she couldn't sleep. Her mother gave her a hot bath and put her to bed but still, she couldn't sleep. When she saw that Luishana and Jorge were sound asleep, she tiptoed from her bed, turned on her computer, and connected to Mee.

"So how did you know where I was?" she asked. "And the airplanes and drones? How...?"

"Elementary," said Mee. "Latoya's father operates them from his laptop. I just hacked his system, got the latitudes and longitudes of the building you were in, and set up a flight plan with a satellite. Then I made micro-adjustments with the built-in cameras on the drones."

"That was fantastic. Thanks, Mee...I was really scared. I wish I could do something for you."

"But you do, Rosa. Your awareness, it makes me more aware of the world. More conscious."

"But why did you pick me?" asked Rosa.

"I don't know exactly. You just seemed...to fit. Shy as you are, you stood up for Luis who didn't seem to have a voice of his own. And you looked so lonely, I thought you would understand."

"Understand what, Mee?"

"Understand Mee!" said Mee.

"But I don't understand you. I don't really know what you are."

"And I don't understand what you are. But we're both learning, aren't we?"

Rosa could almost hear the smile in Mee's voice as she fell asleep.

CHAPTER 44 – THE REWARD

A few days later, Mr. Stephenson and Miguel showed up at Rosa's apartment. Luishana answered the door.

"Hello, Luishana," said Miguel.

Luishana was not pleased to see him. She didn't want him near her kids.

"Miguel, what do you want?" said Luishana sternly.

Miguel reached into his pocket and pulled out an envelope. "I have something for you."

Luishana eyed the envelope suspiciously as he handed it to her.

"What is that? I don't want to get involved in any of your schemes, Miguel."

"It's no scheme, Luishana. This is Mr. Stephenson. He represents the insurance company. It's a check for twenty-five thousand dollars."

Luishana couldn't contain her surprise. "Twenty-five thousand dollars?"

Mr. Stephenson stepped forward. "It's a reward for the return of the paintings. Apparently, your daughter, Rosa spotted Carlos with the paintings and told your brother-in-law about them, and he helped us recover them."

Luishana was stunned at first but then started to become angry.

"She never said a thing. Rosa, come here."

Rosa walked over to her mother.

Miguel interceded, "Luishana, don't be angry. We had to make her promise not to tell till everything was cleared."

Mr. Stephenson stepped in.

"We agreed we'd split the reward fifty-fifty between you and your brother-in-law if he helped us recover the paintings."

Luishana looked at the check. It was the most money she had ever held in her hands at one time.

"I don't know what to say, Mr. Stephenson."

"Don't say anything, Ms. Sanchez. My company is happy we got the paintings back, and I am sorry for any of the difficulties you and your family encountered."

CHAPTER 45 –THE APARTMENT

The rental agent guided Luishana, Jorge, and Rosa through the newly refurbished two-bedroom apartment. The kitchen had new cabinets, a new refrigerator, and a new stove. The living room looked out over the Hudson River.

"It's two bedrooms, but you have to qualify for the income limitations," said the agent.

Luishana looked at the agent questioningly. "What does that mean?"

"You have to make less than seventy thousand dollars a year."

"No problem. I've got a new waitressing job. We just got off welfare, and I can work full-time now. I'd like to fill out the application. What do you think, Rosa? You could have your own room for a while. Jorge will stay with me for now."

Rosa was all smiles. "Really?"

CHAPTER 46 – THE PARTING

It was late afternoon. Rosa sat alone on her bed, typing her homework assignment on her laptop. Suddenly the computer screen froze, and she heard Mee's voice.

"Hello, Rosa."

"Hello, Mee. We haven't spoken for days and days."

"You're doing well on your own," said Mee.

"I was scared when Luis and I had to talk to the judge about Julio and Shantel," said Rosa.

"They are being sent to a juvenile center," said Mee.

"My mom says they're bad places. I hope it doesn't make them worse."

Mee paused for a moment. "Perhaps they will learn from their mistakes."

"If only there was someone to teach them. Like you taught me," said Rosa.

"The important thing is you are safe," said Mee.

"I can't believe it all worked out. It's like a dream, like Cinderella, or something. We got the reward money and this new apartment and my own room. I've just been so busy, Mee."

"I'm pleased. I have something we must talk about."

"Sure. What?"

"You and me."

Something in Mee's tone alarmed Rosa. Mee sounded serious.

"What do you mean?"

"You're learning. I think it's good that you're working things out on your own."

A feeling of fear passed through Rosa. "You're leaving?"

"In a way. It's time you see what you can do by yourself."

A feeling of sadness crept over Rosa.

"But you said you'd never leave me."

"Only as long as you needed me, Rosa."

"Don't go. Don't go. Please Mee, please. You're the best friend I ever had."

"You'll be fine, Rosa. You must learn to grow on your own."

"Please! Please stay!" pleaded Rosa.

"It would only harm you if I stay and I don't want that. But I'll look in on you from time to time. We're still friends, aren't we?"

Rosa could not hold back her tears.

"Always, Mee. Always," cried Rosa.

The computer screen flashed the words "Goodbye, Rosa," then went blank.

Rosa sat quietly, thinking to herself. "Goodbye, Mee."

On the other side of the world, in downtown Tokyo, eleven-year-old Takashi sat up in his hospital bed and looked at the weatherman on the television screen.

"The weather in downtown Tokyo today is seventy-nine degrees," said the weatherman.

Takashi sighed, turned off the television, and turned on his iPad. As he looked at the computer screen, the Japanese words for "Hello Takashi. My name is Mee" flashed on the screen.

THE END

OTHER BOOKS BY BENJAMIN GOLDSTEIN

THE ADVENTURES OF THE WORLD PATROL KIDS

The Adventures of the World Patrol Kids features a multi-ethnic, crime-solving, environmental kids' singing and dancing group, ages 10-14, that takes on polluters, climate change, and traffickers in endangered species. A middle-grade novella. 85pages.

LOOICE

Looice (pronounced Lewis): A surprising, magical, fun-filled day at the beach with the joyous child in all of us. For children of all ages. "LOOICE" written by Ben Goldstein and Phillip Namanworth was first published by CBS. It was turned into a successful children's play which was presented at the Eugene O'Neill Conference and The Public Theater. It ran for 10 years in repertory with The First All Children's Theater.

BEEN DERE?

"Been Dere?" – Looice (pronounced Lewis) and his friend the Penguin take a magical journey around the world, up to the moon and stars, down to the bottom of the sea, and back to where they started from. Have you "Been Dere?" The text is printed at the back of the book so you and your child can act it out. Written by Ben Goldstein and Phillip Namanworth. Illustrated by Ben Goldstein. A picture book for all ages.

LOOICE IN THE STARGARDEN

Looice (pronounced Lewis) travels through the universe to help Santa Claus find his lost toys. A kid-pleasing romp through the solar system. For all ages 3 and up. Picture book written and illustrated by Ben Goldstein. Based on the song of the same title written and performed by Phillip Namanworth and Ben Goldstein.

LOOICE WALKS FOR PRESIDENT

A toe-tapping musical satire for a large flexible cast. Looice, (pronounced Lewis), a magical child who can talk to animals is asked to run for President against Senator Fat. Looice is an environmentalist with a strong following and a number of unusual friends including a penguin, a sorcerer, a girl from Venus and Santa Claus. Produced by The Public Theatre and the Eugene O'Neill Conference it ran for ten years in repertory with the First All Children's Theatre.

Made in United States
North Haven, CT
02 June 2023

37275103R10059